Sandra

Euphemia Chukwu

Published by
Fame Star Media
Unit 7, Studio Court
28 Lawrence Road
South Tottenham
London
N15 4ER

+447446234704
Website: www.famestaragency.com
Email: info@famestaragency.com

ISBN: 978-0-9957695-0-2

For more copies, feedback or questions, you can reach the author on:

www.famestaragency.com
www.facebook.com/euphemia.chu
www.facebook.com/Theladyfame
www.twitter.com/euphemiachukwu
www.linkedin.com/in/euphemia-chukwu
www.instagram.com/meuphemia

Chapter One

The Hang Over

"Mmm! my head; where am I?" I mumbled as I gently opened my foggy eyes to look around; pain engulfed my head — I dared not move; so I closed them again. It must have been four hours on, I can't be certain. My head was throbbing and my body ached. I knew I had to open my eyes no matter how much it was hurting; with all the strength I could muster, I lifted up my head and forced my eyes open. Big mistake! The bright light shot through my eyes; either I or the room started spinning; then there was a churn in my stomach.

"Oh no..." I muttered as I ran out of bed as fast as I could and dashed straight into the washroom. I barely managed to lift up the toilet seat cover before I let rip and threw up until it felt like my gut would come out. When I finished, I slouched to the ground feeling drained.

"I am never drinking again," I murmured.

After few minutes or so, I pulled myself up to the sink, holding to it as if my life depended on it. My shoulders drooped and my head was down in defeat. I looked up slowly in the mirror and didn't like what I saw. My hair was scanty as if I just got electrocuted — well almost. My eyes were swollen and red with the smudged black mascara and the smeared brazen red lipstick; I looked like something out of a horror movie. I turned on the tap letting the cold water run for a while; the sound of the running water was a pounding knock to my head. With unsteady hands, I scooped the water and splashed on my face. "Aaahh," I sighed feeling slightly relieved and refreshed; the cold water felt so good on my hot face. I decided to drench my whole body as well in the tub when suddenly there was a knock at the door; the shock of it jolted me almost against the wall.

"Are you alright?" I heard a male voice ask.

A look of terror defined my face. For a moment I panicked. Who was that and what was he doing in my flat? My heart began to race. The voice came again, "Are you alright in there?"

For some reason, and the only thing I thought best at the time to do: I ran to the door pressing my body against it.

"Yeah, I'm fine…fine thanks," I stammered.

"Would you want a glass of water?" He questioned.

"No, no, I'm fine, thanks," I replied.

"Okay," he said with an unconvinced tone but he left me alone to my relief. I quickly turned around shutting my eyes as tight as I could and trying to remember what happened the previous night.

At that moment so many thoughts ran through my mind; one thing was certain: everything I was feeling early on seemed to have vanished only to be replaced by panic and fear.

"Think, think," I said slapping my forehead in frustration as I contemplated; 'Who is that stranger in my flat? What was he doing here? How did he get in?' Then it occurred to me, 'Okay...I must have met him last night, right? Did I? Oh no, please don't tell me I...' I pleaded that something else other than what I was thinking happened.

"Think, think, oh!" groaning and rubbing my face roughly with both hands as more thoughts ran through my mind.

'I might have met the man in my flat last night; I might have slept with him; oh! no, did we use protection?'

"Oh! God, please help me," I cried out ashamed of myself and bitterly disappointed.

"Okay," I said trying to compose myself; I walked back to the sink, washed my face quickly, brushed my teeth and finger brushed my hair. Once I was satisfied with the way I looked, I took a deep breath and said, "Well, you are not going to get any answers here; he sounds like a reasonable guy." With a stern look at myself in the mirror, I convinced myself, "Go get some answers girl!"

I took another deep breath, shook my hair and opened the door heading straight to my bedroom. There in my bed lying down naked, only half covered, was a ruggedly handsome-looking man with a big grin on his face like the cat that got the cream. At that moment all my fears were confirmed: another one-night stand, only that this time, I couldn't remember anything.

'I am really never going to drink again,' I thought.

He extended a hand and motioned me back to bed. Tempting as it was with his seductive dark brown eyes, I just wanted him to leave my flat. With a fake smile, I reached out for my negligee on the chair near my bed to cover my sexy black French lace chemise. Before I could get it, he grabbed my hand and pulled me back to bed, rolled on top of me and started kissing me passionately on the lips. With a very little attempt to fight him off, I gave in to the passion, hating myself for it.

But he was such a great kisser; what is a girl to do? He ran his hand slowly up my legs, to my thighs as far as it could go, moving his soft lips gently to my neck all the way to my breasts. I groaned in excitement. In the height of the passion, I could hear the phone ringing. I tried to ignore it but the persistent ringing was a distraction to me; a welcomed distraction. I pushed him to stop so I could go and answer the phone. "Leave it," he murmured, still kissing me while trying to get me back in the mood. I started to relax and get back into it but the phone won't stop ringing.

"I have to get it; it might be important," I urged pushing him off with more force this time and dashed to the phone.

As I ran into the living room to get the phone, I could see on the floor trails of our clothing we wore the previous night. I saw two empty wine glasses on the table and an empty bottle of Chardonnay on the floor with some kebab wraps crunched up near the glasses. I felt nauseous again but the tenacious ringing of the phone caused me not to dwell on it. I grabbed the handset of the phone from the side table by the 62-inch plasma television set while reaching up to open the window for some fresh air.

4

"Hello?"

"Hello Sandra," Mandy chuckled cheekily.

"Hey Mandy, am I glad to hear from you?" I sighed slumping down on my creamy leather settee not minding that it was cold against my skin. As a matter of fact, I relished it as I needed to cool off — if you know what I mean. The sensation of his soft tender kisses went up and down my body like electrical pulses with my mind gravitating towards him by the minute, then I shook my head to clear the image from my mind and focused on the conversation.

"Sure you are; is he still there?" she queried with utmost curiosity. I pretended to not have heard or know what she was talking about.

"The weather is so lovely today," I commented vaguely trying to change the subject. "Sandy!" She screamed at me in frustration. Laughing softly I whispered, "Is who still here?" taunting her some more but at the same time wanting to know if she knew who the man in my bed was, as my memory of last night was still hazy.

"Hunky Jake, of course!" she exclaimed.

"Jake," I echoed slowly with vacuous expression.

"You don't remember last night, do you?" she surmised not really surprised.

"No, I don't!" I admitted swinging my legs from the sofa and sitting upright. "I have been throwing up all morning and then found a stranger in my bed."

"You were mixing and knocking your drinks back last night. I had to put you in a cab to make sure you get home safe. I wanted to come but I couldn't tear you away from Jake. I can't say I blame you because the guy is hot; but then you always get the hot guys. Tell me everything and leave nothing out," she demanded. Shaking my head and laughing gently, I said, "Can't talk now; he's still here. I tell you one thing though: he is a great kisser."

"I gathered that much since you spent the whole night with your tongue down his throat," she broke in jokingly.

"Very funny. I hope I did not ignore you all night. It was supposed to be girls' night out", I recalled. "What happened to Tracy and Joanne?"

"Joanne got off with Mick, Jake's friend. I was getting on so well with him but as soon as I went to the toilet, I came out and found the two of them snogging their face off; she is a cow!" She pointed out still peeved.

"Oh Mandy! I'm so sorry," I said sympathetically.

"You know what she's like; anyway she went home with him. As for Tracey, she was pukey and cried all night. As you know, she can't handle her drinks so I had to make sure she got home alright," she said.

"Sandra, are you coming back to bed?" Jake called out from my bedroom. Covering the mouthpiece of the phone, I yelled back, "Just a minute!" Removing my hand from the mouthpiece I said mischievously, "Got to go. Jake is missing me."

"Oh, you bad girl you," she joked laughing.

"I will call you later and fill you in with all the gory details," I said giggling.

"You better," she replied also giggling.

"Love you, babe," I said.

6

"Me too," she replied dropping the phone. I left the handset on the glass table, looked around my very messy sitting room and let out a deep breath thinking of the cleaning up I have to do. I looked up at the glass wall clock; it was two o'clock in the afternoon. Shocked by how late it was, I jumped up to my feet and made my way back to my room. Jake still stretched out on the bed waiting for me and asked, "Is everything alright?"

"Yeah, but we have to end it; it's two o'clock and I have a lot to do today," I said putting on my negligee.

"Can't we have five more minutes?" he pleaded.

"No. I'm afraid I can't. I really do have a full day," I insisted hastening him from the bed. He stood up fully naked. I could not help but gaze at the beauty of this specimen of a man standing before me. My body was calling out to him but I knew if I responded, we would not leave my room that day and I really had things to do. I tightened my negligee and picked up his t-shirt and threw it at him, "Come on. Get dressed." Reluctantly, he started to dress up and I went back to the living room to tidy up.

By 2:30 pm, Jake was ready to go and my living room were looking much better, he took his wallet from the glass table and said, "I don't want to leave you," drawing me closer.

"I know," I replied, pulling away from him and heading towards the door. When we reached the front door, I opened it for him to leave.

"Can I see you again?" he asked holding my hand and looking into my eyes.

"Sure," I answered looking away.

"Can I have your number?" He requested.

"I'll call you," I promised with a half-hearted smile.

He took out his wallet and gave me his business card. We kissed passionately at the door saying goodbye because I had no intention of seeing him again and I was quite certain he knew that I wouldn't. As he walked off, he turned around looking pitiful. I waved at him and he waved back then continued walking. I closed the door and let out a sigh of relief running my fingers through my hair. I headed straight to my bedroom to sleep; I still had a few hours more before meeting up with the girls later. Upon entering my room, I looked up at the heart-shaped clock on the wall; the time was 2:35 pm. I opened the window wide and a light cool breeze hit my face. I closed my eyes and took in the fresh fragrance of summer flowers. I crawled into bed and shut my eyes still smelling Jake's cologne on the pillow. I drifted off to sleep.

I woke up a couple of hours later and after a warm shower, I was feeling much better and a lot more clearheaded. I had my coffee, called Anthony briefly, and then Mandy. I spoke to her for about forty-five minutes catching up about last night and getting excited about the forthcoming fun night. On ending the call, I went to get ready.

Playing in the background on the radio was my favourite song, *Girls Just Wanna Have Fun* by Cyndi Lauper. I turned it up and sang along as I brushed my hair and put the finishing touch on my makeup. I was feeling excited about the night. Since it was Saturday, I decided to go with the look of the scarlet woman. I slipped into my short, red, sexy cleavage-cut designer dress by Fame Star over my black and red lingerie, then my black shoes by Christian Louboutin finishing off with my black handbag by Valentino.

Flicking my hair back, I took one last look in the mirror. Pleased with my appearance, I picked up the Gucci watch Anthony bought for me last Christmas from my dressing table and placed on my wrist. I took a quick glance at the watch and it was time to go. I looked out from the window to check if the taxi had arrived; he was just pulling up.

The taxi driver was a middle-aged, dark-brown-haired man with traces of gray. He had a warm and kind face which lit up as soon as he saw me approaching. "Are you the one that called for a taxi to Biancone Italian Restaurant?" He asked smiling and hoping I was the one. "Yes," I replied getting inside the cab at the back seat. Not long after I got in, Mandy called to know where I was; then Tracey, to let me know that she would be picking up Joanne with her car. The taxi pulled up outside the restaurant and Mandy was there waiting. I paid the driver and rushed out of the cab as Mandy got up and walked towards me. We hugged and air kissed both cheeks. We admired and commented on each other's outfits. I didn't even notice the cab as it drove away.

Mandy looked stunning in her elegant black V-neckline short cocktail dress by Jovani, a designer shoe, and handbag by Fendi with her dark sunglasses from Gucci. She looked like a movie star. She always liked going over the top. Far gone are the years she used to wear glasses and pigtails — yes, she would very much like to forget.

Mandy and I had been friends from our school days; we had so much in common that we concluded we must have been

9

twins separated at birth. But, of course, it wouldn't matter that I am a 5ft 8" and Mandy is a 5ft 4" though we both have great figures. She always wore the highest heels she could find just to look like a supermodel.

"Exotic, sultry and smouldering, I mean, you are strikingly beautiful. Your long dark hair, big brown eyes, and enviable curves, I need to make sure I keep up," she emphasised. "The pressure of being a friend of a supermodel is quite high. I have to make sure I live up to it," and she does.

Mandy's long brown hair was parted to create a beautiful appearance on her round-shaped face. She was a pretty girl with a quirky and wonderful personality, very loyal, and dependable in times of need.

We went to the restaurant to wait for Joanne and Tracey. As always, heads turned as we walked by. A handsome Italian waiter attended to us and showed us to our table. As we soaked up the ambiance of the place, Tracey and Joanne arrived. The same waiter brought them to our table. Tracey, bless her, was the most sensible and plain-looking; she was just a little bit bigger than the three of us.

She had long blond hair which she always wore tied back no matter what she was wearing. She wore glasses, too. She had been in the same relationship with her fiancé, John, for four years but she always had time for us. She appeared to be timid but she had a strong personality. She attended church every Sunday and had been trying to get us to go with her but we had never been serious about it. Joanne claimed to be an atheist though she didn't even know what it meant. She said the only time she would go to church was when she was getting married or when any of us was. I attended a few times with Anthony, Tracey, and Mandy, but I never got serious about it. I felt like I was not good enough to be there.

Everyone loved Tracey. There was something peaceful about her. The lovely long fl oral white dress she chose for the night looked good on her. Joanna, on the other hand, was in constant competition with me in every way. For instance, she called me early on to find out what I was wearing for the night. I, however, misinformed her that I was wearing a pink dress. If I had told her red, she would've been in red, too. As she sat down opposite me, she glared at me as she tightened her lips. I pretended I didn't notice. She looked great in what she was wearing but she would have preferred wearing a red outfit. Joanne could be very competitive and overly assertive. She stood up and wriggled her hip in her very short mini dress as to be noticed by everyone. "Waiter, bring us three bottles of your finest c hampagne," s he called out in a grandiloquent and boastful manner. Slightly embarrassed by her lack of tact, we rolled our eyes. The waiters didn't seem to mind as their eyes were fixed at our table. Joanne sat back down. Noticing my Valentino handbag, she quickly showed us her new and latest collection from Chanel and shoe to match.

"Daddy bought them for me. Do you like them?" She boasted.

Her Alexander McQueen silk short mini dress clung to her small body frame of size ten. I couldn't help but admire the dress. She noticed me watching and with a satisfied grin, she fl icked her curly blond bob-styled hair cut away from her blue eyes.

11

Tracey and Mandy laughed. Mandy started talking about our waiter and how handsome he was; we all agreed. Tracey just smiled. The waiter, Marco, was every bit the Italian stallion. As he poured our champagne, Tracey covered her glass in refusal. We all knew why she refused to drink. One: she couldn't handle her drinks; two: she had church the Sunday and she never missed it. She ordered a bottle of sparkling water instead; we all looked at her and giggled playfully. We held up our glasses and toasted to "girls who wanna have fun, minus one," we mocked Tracey.

"That's not fair, I like to have fun," she protested.

"Don't worry. We still love you," I said mischievously as I gave her a hug with my left hand. Joanne and I downed our glass of champagne. We both laughed as the bubble went up to our noses.

The evening was filled with banter as we drank and ate. After our meal, we were given complimentary liquor which went down well. Joanne insisted that she would pay for the meal as she took out her credit card. "Daddy's plastic always comes in handy," she said brashly.

"What club are we hitting tonight then?" queried Mandy.

"Not the one we went to last night; I can't risk bumping into Jake," I objected.

"Mmm, Mick was a disappointment if you know what I mean. Can you believe he fell asleep on me?" Joanne whispered with embarrassment.

Mandy and I burst out laughing while Tracey let out a weak smile. Joanne recoiled into her seat sulking.

"It serves you right for stealing him away from me," complained Mandy.

Joanne interrupted in protest but before it escalated, Tracey quietened them both in order to prevent an argument.

"What about the club you guys went to last Friday?" She suggested.

"You guys agreed it was good. I can drop you off before I head home and don't bother to try and talk me into coming; you know I don't like clubbing and going to bars. I only went yesterday because it was Joanne's birthday and she begged me to come."

"And I really appreciate it, darling," Joanne said warmly. Leaving a large tip for the waiters, we made our way out of the restaurant. As we were leaving, Marco handed his phone number to me. I thought to myself, "What is it with me and Italian men?" Breaking my thoughts, Mandy bumped my shoulder and smirked.

Tracey dropped us off outside the club. After kisses to her, we waved her goodnight. The three of us linked arms with excitement and went inside the club. The club was not yet too busy as it was only 11 pm. Joanne ordered for champagne to be brought to our table. Whilst we waited for the drinks to arrive, we scouted the joint. We noticed some football players in the VIP section motioning us to join them. Mandy wanted to go; Joanne and I weren't keen. There was a thirty-something-year-old businessman checking out Joanne; she seemed interested but when she saw I was not showing any interest, she was no longer interested.

Our champagne arrived and we toasted to a fun night. Though I declared never to drink again; with the girls, it wasn't going to be easy to keep that promise. But I was mindful to take it easy that night as I'd had a heavy night the night before — anyway, I did that whenever I had a terrible hangover.

A while later, the gentleman who was checking out Joanne sent over a bottle of champagne. The club got busier and we were ready to hit the dance floor. I did not want to drink champagne anymore as that got me drank faster so I went to the bar to buy Vodka and Lemonade. As I was about to pay the bartender, I heard a voice behind me say, "I'll get that." I turned around to put a face on the voice as he handed over the money to the bartender. It was an attractive-looking man with blond hair.

"I'm Aden," he introduced stretching out his hand for a handshake.

"Sandra," I responded, shaking his hand. "Thanks for the drink."

"No problem. Would you like to dance?" He asked. Smiling, I agreed to dance with him. We danced for a while together then I danced over to the girls who were also on the dance floor. Aden followed me so I introduced him briefly to them though I doubt they heard me because the music was really loud. We all danced until we were tired. We then went and sat down and had more drinks. Towards the end of the night, we had drunk, danced, and had been chatted up by different men. It became clear to Aden I was not interested in him. I wasn't really into blonds. I was more of a dark-haired kind of girl but Mandy seemed to like him so I introduced them and they got on well. They ended up together at the end of the night so after the club, she went home with him. Joanne was determined to make up for her lack of success last night and went home with some guy she was practically making out with on the dance floor. As for me, though I danced with different men and kissed a few, I was resolute about not going home with anyone. I got home about 5 am, kicked off my shoes, slipped out of my dress, crashed on my bed, and fell asleep.

The phone rang and woke me up about mid-day; it was Joanne, all bright and chirpy. She couldn't wait to give me all the low-down of her conquest. I tried to listen but I was still sleepy. After going on for what seemed like hours, she finally inquired whether I went home with anyone. When I informed her I didn't, it pleased her greatly. She proceeded to brag about how many gifts she got from her very wealthy parents. When she had finished, she asked me if we could meet for a drink later. I must say I had never met anyone who drank as much as Joanne and she never suffered a hangover. I, on the other hand, was not able to swerve it.

"Why do I put myself through this time and time again?" I asked myself.

I made up some insubstantial excuse to get out of this one; the thought of having another drink was making my stomach queasy. I suggested she went with the man she met the night but she snorted and asked whether I was joking because I knew she wouldn't want to see him again. I laughed out loud feeling more awake. I asked her if she had spoken to Mandy yet and she said she was going to call her next. After a few more banter we said goodbye. I stretched lazily on the bed recollecting all the activities of the night and the night before; smiling halfheartedly, I thought for a moment about Anthony and wondered if I should call him, but then he probably was going to be at church. I decided to get out of bed. I took a shower and washed my hair to get rid of the cigarette smell. I then changed my bed sheets.

After changing, I cooked something to eat, cleaned up the house then slouched on the settee turning on the television. I flicked through the channels not finding anything interesting to watch. I decided to call Mandy to find out about her night with Aden. The phone rang once and she answered as I got surprised and curious all the same. Before I could speak, she declared she was about to call me sounding all excited. "She must have had a very good night," I thought. We chatted for a couple of hours and she gave me every detail of her night leaving nothing out; then she squealed excitedly and said, "Did I tell you that Aden is a footballer?" Surprised by this revelation, I sat up and replied, "No…" Before I could finish, she cut in enthusiastically.

"Yeah, he plays for one of the top clubs," gasping in delight. "His house is gigantic. Did I mention his house is gigantic? It is even bigger than Joanne's house."

She went on and on about the house and how wonderful Aden is and so on. I didn't really get a chance to talk much as she was on cloud nine. Just before hanging up, she said, "Thanks."

"What for?" I asked.

"For introducing him to me," she replied.

"He wasn't my type," I added.

"Must go, darling, speak to you during the week. I love you lots," she declared.

16

After talking to Mandy, I wondered why Aden didn't tell me he was a footballer — not that it would have made any difference to me, anyway. I was pleased that I introduced him to Mandy and I hoped that it wasn't going to be a night's stand. At the same time, I was worried for her and prayed that he did not hurt her.

My Little Girl

My life had taken many twists and turns so much that I could not trace to which road led me here; a life that I wish I was not leading yet one that I couldn't bring myself to bail.

My mind drifted back in the memory lane to do a bit of soul-searching.

Islington in North London where it all began; the one-bedroom council flat I used to live in with Grandma Faye. As people went in and out, I tried hard to remember my life here but I couldn't recall much; I began crying and thinking about Grandma and her kind smile. I remembered her warm cuddles and soft brown hair with streaks of gray tickling my nose whenever I got the horrible nightmares and cuddled up to her. She would always sing me to sleep or tell me the story of God's little princess who was loved more than anything in this world and how God always watched over her and never left or let anything bad happen to her because she was so special to Him; then she would say a prayer and kiss me on my forehead. Every Sunday, she made sure we went to church and she would tell me stories from the Bible. At the end of every story, she would say, "You must always be good to people and work hard in everything you do so that you will have a good life and still be God's little princess."

I loved her so much. Even though I was only eight years old, it felt like my world had come to an end when she died. In her belongings, there was a letter addressed to my name with the written instruction: "To be opened the day after my 21st birthday." I kept that letter safe over the years as it was the only thing I had left of her. The day after my 21st birthday during the night when I was free from a hangover, I brought the letter out to Anthony; we just sat there staring at the letter. He asked me if I wanted to be alone to read it; I told him to stay. I was so nervous of what the letter might contain; I asked Anthony to open it. When he opened the letter, there were some pictures in it: one was a picture of Grandma and me when I was about three; the other was a picture of me on the day of my first holy communion dressed in white. I looked so angelic. Grandma died not long after that. The last picture was a painting of a woman with yellow hair and blue eyes and under it was written: "Mama." I wondered if that was my mom. He read the letter out to me:

"To my precious little angel Sandra,
I am so nervous I don't even know where to begin but first of

all, let me wish you a very happy 21st birthday. I wish that I was there to celebrate with you but I know you have turned out to be a wonderful young lady and a true princess of God. I hope you still go to church and say your prayers every day.

Okay, let me start by saying that I love you so very much dear. I want you to know that and never forget it no matter what.

You see, my dear little angel; I am not really your grandma. One night when I finished my cleaning job for one of the rich family houses I worked for every evening in that posh area, Brompton Square, SW3 area, I found you wandering on the streets; you were about two years old and you were covered in blood. I looked around and saw no one looking for you so I took you in. I wanted to take you to the police but I was so scared what they might think so I waited to see if anyone would report you missing but they never did. I listened to the news but never heard anything except the news about the family that got murdered in their home; a father, a mother and their little girl about your age.

Since no one came forward to claim you, I decided I was doing no harm in keeping you and looking after you. You were so scared and refused to talk for months. As I had no children of my own or anyone in the world, I took you in and gave you the name, Sandra. I moved to a different area where no one knew me and I told everyone you were my granddaughter and gave you my surname. Three years later, I watched in the news a missing person's report and there was a picture of you there. It turned out that the body of the little girl who was supposedly murdered alongside members of the family was never found and that little girl is you.

I loved you so much and you were so settled and doing well in school I reasoned with myself that it made no sense destabilising your life and uprooting you. The authorities would only put you in care since you had no mom and dad. Nobody came forward to claim you so I did not say anything though I was scared someone might recognise you; funny enough, no one ever said a thing. Although some people cast the odd look here and there, it all passed. I didn't want you to carry this burden of knowledge until you had finished school then you can decide on what to do. I hope this information helps but that's all I remember.

This is a confession of a dying old woman and I hope you can find it in your heart to forgive me. I love you and you will always be my little angel because when you came into my life, you brought light, love, and so much joy. I am so sorry for lying to you. I hoped I would have more time together but I must leave you now when you are ready to, go out there and find out who you are. Always remain strong and whenever you are confused, take it to the Lord in prayer. Surround yourself with godly people and you will never go astray.

Take care, my love, till we meet again someday.

Grandma.

As Anthony read the last line of the letter, tears streamed down my face. He looked at me unsure what to say; he was also shocked by the content of the letter. I could see in his eyes the pity he had for me. I sat there unable to speak; him likewise. So he put the letter down on the table and just hugged me. I burst out crying uncontrollably as he rocked me back and forth stroking my hair lovingly, and comforting me.

Later, I took the letter and the pictures and put them away as if they did not exist and we never spoke of it again.

The next episode of my life took place in Essex where I was adopted by the most loving parents ever. I had uncles and aunties, and cousins and nephews; it was great. I had my own room and in our garden was a swing built for me. Since I was their only child, they doted on me and spoilt me rotten.

After the death of Grandma Faye, I was taken to temporary care. I was there for a few months until Mr. and Mrs. Appleton adopted me. For months, I did not speak and I kept pretty much to myself. The nightmares I used to have returned again. It took me a while before I could accept them as my new family. I was amazed how patient they were with me. I moved to a new school; it was a private school for girls. Mrs. Appleton would always drive me to school every morning and kiss me before I got out of the car. She would always tell me she loved me. She also picked me up after school. Before I went to bed, she would always read me a bedtime story. After, both of them would kiss me goodnight. I felt safe and secure again.

My first Christmas with them was the best Christmas I had ever had. Mr. Appleton dressed up disguising to be Father Christmas but I knew it was him; still, it was fun. Mrs. Appleton woke me up and carried me downstairs to open my presents. As we opened my gifts, I was so excited and happy. For a moment, I forgot about all the sadness and it felt I had always been part of my calling them mom and dad. I just remember them being so happy.

In the morning of my twelfth birthday, mom and dad came to my room singing happy birthday. I was very excited because they were throwing a big party for me at the house. I couldn't wait to see all my friends and cousins. Later on, two of my aunts came to help out with stuff for the party. I went to my room to play with my cousins, Mary and Elizabeth; they were my age too. Mary had long blonde hair to her waist which she loved wearing down. Her hair band was blue which matched her coloured eyes. She looked nice in her blue dress, too.

Elizabeth had brunette hair just like my mom and dad. She had green eyes and loved wearing jeans; she was in blue jeans and yellow top and was a bit of a tomboy. We got on so well they would often come to my house over the weekend for a sleepover and we would stay up practically all night talking and giggling a lot. Mum called out to me and said she and dad were going out to pick up my cake. I ran downstairs, "Why can't dad go on his own?" I asked.

"Because I am also going to pick up a surprise for you after we collect the cake," dad replied pinching my nose gently and playfully.

I gave him a hug looking forward to what my surprise would be. "I love you, dad," I said.

He smiled and said they would be back in an hour's time. I hugged mom and told her I loved her too and that they should hurry back. I watched them get into the silver Mercedes-Benz car; she smiled sweetly and waved as dad drove off. She looked so pretty with her hair up like that. Dad was in his favourite cologne Burberry I bought him for their wedding anniversary the previous month.

Mary called me back upstairs so she could do my hair. I was getting a strange feeling and I couldn't shake it. I kept looking at the time. I became so restless. I had this alarming urge to ring mom, so I did. She picked up and asked if I was alright; I requested to be put through to dad. I inquired if they were both okay; he said they were. They had just collected my birthday cake and were on their way to pick up my surprise. I advised him to drive carefully and that I loved them very much. He told me they loved me too and that I was the best thing that ever happened to them; he said they would be home in thirty minutes; unfortunately, they never came back. I waited and waited and waited at the door until I saw the policemen approach the house; then I knew.

The first thought that came to my mind was, "Not again." Every other thing that happened after that was a blur. From that moment I decided I was not going to let anyone in again; I was never ever going to let my guard down and love anybody because it seemed that anyone that I loved always died. I remember asking Grandma Faye where my mom and dad were and she would say: "They have gone to heaven and that's why you are living with me; you do like living with me, don't you?" I would give her a big hug and a smile shaking my head in delight.

I became cold and uncommunicative; a recluse. Dan and Lily Appleton, my dad's younger brother and his wife, Mary's mom, took me in to live with them. For six months I did not speak to anyone. I started having the same nightmares I used to have when I was younger. As always, the same lady who appeared to me like an angel would sing me to sleep telling me everything was going to be okay and that she loved me. Her voice was so soothing and her eyes filled with love. In my dreams, I would tell her that I want to go with her but she would always say: "Not yet," then she would disappear. For three years I had not seen her in my dreams but after the loss of my mom and dad, I began seeing her every night as I cried myself to sleep. She would comfort me and say to me: "Everything would be alright." All I did was to draw or paint a picture of her. Whenever anyone asked me who she was, I would walk away and say nothing. Finally, Lily had enough of me and they put me back in a foster home and that was the last time I saw them.

In just eleven months, I was placed in eight different foster homes. I still didn't talk to anyone; the more I moved, the more isolated I became. My thirteenth birthday came and went. Not that anyone noticed but I didn't care; I hated birthdays. I hated everyone and everything including myself. I would only wear black clothes with black lipstick and painted my nails black. I never smiled or said anything to anyone. I just wanted to sleep all the time so I could see the blonde beautiful lady that appeared to me in the dream; she was the only one that made me happy.

One night when I was sleeping, she appeared to me as usual. After a while, her face changed and she looked very serious and told me sternly to wake up. When I did, I found one of the boys trying to rape me. I tried to fight him off but he pinned me down. Struggling to fight him off, I pulled a chunk of his blond hair out clutching it in my hand. I then bit his left ear so hard a piece came off. He gave out a loud cry and jumped off screaming, "You freak! I'm going to get you for this; you freak!"

I spat his ear out as some of the other children and the foster caregivers ran to my room. The first thing they noticed was my mouth covered in blood and the piece of the ear on the ground and his hair in my hand. The look of horror and fear that was in their eyes was almost laughable. The boy kept yelling: "She's a freak; I need a doctor. Look what she's done to me. I'm dying! I need a doctor." They tried to find out from me what happened but since I did not tell them, they took his word as he told them that I attacked him when he came to borrow a book from my room. They were about to move me when one of the girls overheard him boasting to his friend how close he was to having me but then I woke up and bit him like a cannibal but next time he would drug me first. After hearing this, she quickly went to the foster caregivers and told them. They moved the boy out and apologised to me. I started to warm up to the girl a bit though I never spoke to her. She took me to parties and introduced me to drinking and boys but they found me to be strange so they stayed away. I started binge drinking; I would go out and stay out all night partying.

One day, the foster caregivers had enough and kicked me out. I was thirteen-and-a-half and not doing well at school. I changed schools five times that year. I was tired of being on my own and feeling unloved. My social worker was tired of my attitude. It was evident she had also given up on me.

I had taken to drinking a lot and was not showing up at school; I couldn't care less about anything. I was in a group home and some of the kids there were pretty messed up: some were high on drugs; others were alcoholics; some others were even prostitutes. One night, one of the girls there died of drug overdose. She was only fifteen. That night, I took a hard look at my life and decided that I would end up like her. I changed my looks back to normal and stopped dressing and looking like Morticia Addams. Everyone stared at me because they had never seen me looking normal before. I even smiled at some of them; they weren't sure what to make of it while some didn't even recognise me. I remembered what Grandma Faye used to say to me: "You must always be good to people and work hard in everything you do so that you will have a good life and still be God's little princess."

The last time I went to church was with her; my adopted parents were not religious. That Sunday, I had the compulsion to go to church. I took the train and went to our old church in Islington. When I got there, everything seemed the same though I was not the same person and it was so strange being there without Grandma. I knelt down and prayed; I asked God to help me to be a better person. I wanted stability in my life. I wanted to be someone that Grandma and my parents would be proud of and to be God's little princess. I didn't want to be lonely anymore. After the church service, I left quietly but my old Sunday school teacher recognised me and stopped me outside.

"Sandra…Sandra Whitley! Is that you?" She called out.

I just smiled at her. I had not said a word to anyone in a year-and-a-half; I was afraid to speak that I didn't see how I could avoid talking to Sister Grace.

"I knew it was you; you look so grown up and pretty. How old are you now? Thirteen…fourteen?" I looked around trying to figure out how to escape the unwanted intrusion; as much as

I tried, there was no way anyone could avoid Sister Grace.

"The last time I saw you were the day of the funeral of your grandmother, Mrs. Whitley. I heard you got adopted by some posh family in Essex. I hope they are treating you well," she said, rubbing my right shoulder.

What a poignant reminder of the death of my parents! I lowered my head sorrowfully.

"What is it, dear? Are you alright?" She asked concerned.

I looked at her as I struggled within me on how to let out the words from my mouth.

"They died in a car crash on my twelfth birthday," I said almost in a whisper.

"Oh, sweet child. I am so sorry," she said grabbing and hugging me tightly.

I did not hug her back. Aware of this as if she knew I was not comfortable with the body contact, she let go of me and cleared her throat.

"Well, it's good to see you again. If you ever need anything please feel free to come to ask. Your grandmother was a good woman. This is my number," she took out a pen and scrap paper from her bag, wrote her number and handed it over to me.

On Monday right after school, I went to my social worker's office. After waiting for a long while for the queue, I walked in to see her. At first, she wasn't too pleased to see me but when she heard what I had to say and my change of appearance, her face lit up. She was so happy and asked me if everything was okay. I expressed my desire to move out of the group home as I was ready to re-join a family if anyone came up. I stated that I wanted to become great in life and I wanted a stable environment where I could study and become a graduate. She was so delighted by what I said. She let down her guard and gave me a hug.

"I will see what I can do; just leave it with me. I'll call you as soon as something comes up," she said smiling.

I left the office feeling positive. In fact, after my visit to the church the previous day, I felt a heavy weight had been lifted off me. I began doing much better in school to the surprise of some of the teachers. As thrilled as they were, they went out of their way to help me. I still kept to myself, studying all the time to catch up with all the work I missed. One sunny afternoon during lunchtime, I sat on my own outside eating my lunch and reading my book, *Pride and Prejudice* by Jane Austen. Not far from me, I could hear some girls shouting. They caught my attention and I looked towards their direction. I could see a girl with long-plaited brown hair and round glasses surrounded by four girls who were calling her names and pushing her around. Of all things, one thing I could not stand was bullying. I had seen enough of that in the foster homes I had been in. She looked so scared; I got up and left my lunch, put the book in my school bag, and walked over to them.

"Is this a private party or can anyone join in?" I asked.

Startled, they all turned around to face me. After sizing me up, one of them came forward.

"Walk away freak girl, this has nothing to do with you," she said. All her friends laughed egging her on.

Walking up to her, I said coldly, "The last person to call me a freak, I bit off his ear and spat it out; he was an older and tougher boy or so he thought. Now, what do you think I should do to you, huh?"

I could see a look of fear in her eyes so I roared at her aggressively; she and her friends scampered. I picked up the girl's school bag from the floor and gave it to her. She took it looking relieved and very grateful.

"They don't look so intimidating now; do they?" I asked smiling at her to get her to relax.

She smiled back and thanked me for helping her. She told me her name was Mandy Gray. I thought she was a new girl in the school but she said she remembered my first day in school. She said I made quite an entrance. She also said that when I walked into the class it was like a scene from a horror movie. Some of the kids started laughing and mocked me asking if I was in the wrong place that it was not a costume party. Mandy said not long after that there were so many rumours going around about me. Some said that I was a cannibal; others said that all I had to do was look at someone and they would disappear amongst other things but not one of them knew anything about me.

From that day on, Mandy stuck with me. She went everywhere with me. I found out we lived in the same neighbourhood. She would often invite me to her house and her parents were always so welcoming and kind to me as if I was one of them. Her twin brothers were so cute though Mandy thought they were annoying. I loved her family for their closeness; they reminded me of my parents. I loved spending time at theirs. Mandy also had an older sister, Angela, who was in the university. All Mandy ever talked about was how she wanted to follow in her sister's footsteps and become a doctor. She asked me what I wanted to be; I told her I wasn't sure then. She would say that I should become a famous actress or a supermodel because I was so pretty and tall. She said if she was as beautiful as I was, she would definitely be a supermodel.

Three months after I went to visit my social worker, she came around to the group home and asked me how I was getting on. After, she smiled and said she had found me a new foster family. She told me how nice they were and that they had an older girl living with them as well and that I would settle in nicely. I was so excited I didn't know when I leaped on her and gave her a big hug. I asked her when I would move in and she said as soon as I was ready. She also reassured me that I would not be changing school because it was just two bus rides away to my school. I was so happy I knew that was my second chance of a normal family and to make something of my life.

I thanked God for answering my prayers and I promised to work very hard in school and to be the best that I could be.

Everything was looking up. I seemed to be catching the eyes of a lot of boys in and out of school which surprised me though Mandy kept saying that I was very pretty; I seemed to be the only one who was unaware of it. A boy from a year ahead of me in school came up to me one day and asked Mandy if she could excuse us; as Mandy was about to go, I told her to stay.

"You can say whatever you have to say to me in her presence," I said to him.

He looked around nervously, "Umm, would you like to go out sometime to catch a movie or something?" He asked.

Mandy nudged me in excitement to say yes.

"I don't go out with strangers," I replied.

Mandy opened her eyes wide amazed that I turned him down.

"Well, that can easily be fixed. I'm Mark Evans and this is my final year in school. I have wanted to ask you out for about six months now but I have been a bit of a coward wondering what people might say. I was also scared that you would not give me a hearing. Every time I look at you, there is always such sadness in your eyes. I would literally walk past you and you would not notice me. I just want to be given the chance to get to know you more. Plus, you are the hottest girl in the entire school. I would really love it if you can be my date for the school ball. I promise to tell you more about myself," he said almost pleading with me.

I glanced over at Mandy who was shaking her head in agreement. I then looked across and saw a group of boys watching us so I asked him if they were his friends. He told me they were.

"I suppose if I turn you down now, it would be quite humiliating, right?" I asked.

He looked pessimistic. Mandy looked at me then at him then back at me again. Unable to control herself, she burst out in excitement.

"Come on, Sandra! Give him a chance. He is the hottest guy in school; it makes sense that the hottest girl in school should go out with the hottest guy. Besides, all the girls are dreaming of just one date with him."

"Then I guess he better goes and ask one of them out," I said walking off.

He ran in front of me apologising for what Mandy said and told me he was not really bothered about all that; he just wanted us to get to know each other as friends then see what happens. I agreed to go out with him with one condition: that one of his friends must ask Mandy to be their date for the ball too which they did by the end of the day. Mark and I started dating and became the hottest couple in school. Sudden, my popularity shot up and everyone liked me. I lost my virginity to Mark; it was his first too; I was sixteen and he was seventeen. We were together up until he left school and went to the university.

We started to drift apart but before that, his elder brother who did modelling kept telling me I was very beautiful and would make a great model; so he introduced me to his agent, Marcy, and she got me a job almost immediately. Mark was not too happy that I was spent so much time with his brother for my modelling career. His brother and I went on some photo shoots few times and Mark accused us of sleeping together. I got fed up with the accusations. I slept with his brother to spite him but I hated myself afterward. I wanted to tell him but Mandy said it would not be a good idea.

Mr. and Mrs. Abbott seemed like lovely people. Francesca, their daughter, was a bit cold towards me but I figured she needed time to adjust and get used to having a new girl in the family. I guess it couldn't be easy having to share a room with someone new when she was used to having the room all to herself. For the first time in a long time, I felt settled. I was earning a lot of money from my modelling but I wanted to focus more on my education so I turned down a lot of jobs; Mrs. Abbott was very supportive. Everything was going great. I was no longer having the nightmares or seeing the beautiful blonde lady with blue eyes.

Anthony Wilson

I remember when we first met. It was early summer on a Friday afternoon; the weather was really hot. Mandy and I were coming back from Six Form College. We stopped by to buy some booze for later as we always did on Fridays. In the shop was this gorgeous-looking older guy in his twenties; he was tall, dark, muscular and really hot in his shorts and loose blue vest; you could tell that he worked out a lot. I was practically drooling over him; so was Mandy. We thought he was so cool; I just had to have him and when Sandra wanted a man, Sandra would get him. I learned from an early age that men seemed to be drawn to me and pretty much tripped over themselves to do or give me what I wanted.

Men started noticing me from an early age; too early for my liking. Mandy and I started giggling until he noticed us checking him out. He looked over few times which gave me the green light to approach him with boldness. As he was about to pay for his bottle of water, I walked over to him at the counter.

"And a bottle of vodka, please; he is paying," I said to the cashier casually looking up and smiled sweetly at the hunk standing next to me.

He lifted his eyebrow with his mouth opened as he marvelled at my impudent manner. Our eyes locked for a moment; letting out a slight smile, he said, "I guess I am."

The cashier brought the large bottle of vodka and he paid. I took the bottle and walked off leaving him there.

"Wait!" He called after me.

I ignored him and kept on walking towards Mandy who was waiting for me; I flashed my teeth at her smiling broadly. We walked out and he caught up with us just outside the shop and said to me with a hint of annoyance in his tone, "What...is that it?"

"What?" I asked acting like I had no idea of what he was referring to.

"So do you do this often?" He asked smiling.

Wow! He had the most beautiful sexy smile I had ever seen with his perfect white teeth.

"Only to the hot guys," I replied flirtatiously.

"So you think I'm hot?" He asked flirting with me too as we shared a moment.

"Okay...okay, break it up," said Mandy, pushing us apart a tad. "Mandy is the name and I am a lawyer; well, I will be and this is my best friend, Sandra, who you've already met. She is a supermodel. So what's your name?" she asked seductively.

Clearing his throat, he replied, "My name is Anthony; Anthony Wilson. I am a doctor."

Mandy and I looked at each other and pulled a face.

"Well, Mr. Anthony Wilson...doctor, you are taking us out for a drink tonight," I said boldly.

"What if I am busy tonight?" He asked.

"Cancel it," I said flirtatiously handing him my mobile phone number then kissed him on the lips making sure my breasts pushed against his chest. We said goodbye to him and left.

He called me thirty minutes later. We spoke for a while and arranged on the venue and time to meet. We spoke until I got home.

I went to Mandy's to get ready before we went out for the night. We drank half a bottle of the vodka he bought for us early on. We were feeling jolly and ready for a good night. We went to a pub in the west-end; afterward, we went on to a club. We had a brilliant time. Anthony was a fantastic kisser and a great dancer. All the girls in the club checked him out. He looked yummy in his Hugo Boss shirt and black trouser and he smelt good in his Kelvin Klein aftershave. Mandy got off with some guy but Anthony took both of us home like a gentleman. The next day, he called to see if we were okay. We arranged to meet up for a drink in the afternoon for just him and me.

After we had a quick drink, I requested to see where he lived so we went back to his place. It was a nice flat, clean and tidy. We started kissing and fondling and before I could say Jack, were in his bedroom. He took out a condom which I helped him put on. We started kissing again as I sat on top of him on the bed; he rolled me on my back. He was so gentle and loving.

He took me home afterward requesting to see me the next day. I told him I had college. He was taken aback that I was still in school. I told him that I was seventeen and asked if that was going to be a problem for him leaning over and kissing him provocatively to which he replied: 'No'.

I got out of the car and waved goodbye.

The summer holidays was great. Anthony, Mandy and I spent a lot of time together. The following year was going be our last year in college before we go to university so we had to buckle down and work hard. I spent a lot of time at Mandy's doing my course work. I tried to spend as little time as I could at home. I couldn't wait to be eighteen and get out of that hell hole. If I wasn't at Mandy's studying, I would be at the library and by the time I got in, it would be late — not that it made much difference to Mr. Abbott, my foster dad.

New Year's Eve was brilliant. Anthony got us some tickets to a posh club where we met Joanne. Mandy and I were on the dance floor having such a great time while Anthony went to buy the drinks. Joanne joined us, we danced and danced until the music changed to a slow song. Mandy and I went back to Anthony; she followed us.

"We haven't introduced ourselves. I am Joanne Fairfax, daughter of Maxwell Fairfax," she announced expecting us to know who her father was.

Since we were not impressed, she proceeded to ask our names.

"My name is Sandra, this is Mandy and Anthony, my boyfriend," I said holding him close to which he responded by giving me a kiss on the head.

"Come and join us on our table; we have just ordered some champagne," she said optimistically.

"Maybe later. Anthony just got us drinks," I replied.

"Do you mind then if I stay with you guys? My friends are a bit of a bore. I'll just get my drink," she said.

As she left to get her drink, the three of us shared a look then a song came on that Anthony and I liked so we went dancing and holding each other close enough. The dance was pretty raunchy as we started to snog. After dancing for a while, we went back to our seat where Mandy and Joanne were drinking a bottle of champagne she brought over from her table. After finishing my vodka and lemonade, I joined them in drinking the champagne which Joanne kept ordering. She did not return to her friends; she stayed with us the rest of the night. She was nice, a bit flashy but fun. By the end of the night after guzzling down so much champagne especially Mandy and Joanne, we were pretty drunk, not Anthony though, he didn't really drink that much. I figured sometimes he only drank to please me. Joanne said her driver would drop us all home and she invited us to a New Year's Day party at hers later on in the evening. She said her driver would pick us up. We exchanged numbers and went home.

The phone woke us up about midday. I was reluctant to pick up but the caller was persistent.

"Answer it," grumbled Anthony nudging me.

Lazily, I reached for my phone on the bed table, "Hello," I murmured still half asleep.

"Hi, it's me, Joanne," she said all chirpy and loud.

"Who?" I asked still dissipating from last night.

"Joanne, we met in the club last night; remember? Anyway, you need to text me your address so the driver would come and pick you up for the party about 5 pm. I know you're still sleeping so I will see you later okay, ta- ta," she said all happy and bouncy putting the phone down. I put the handy down and went back to sleep.

There was a knock at the door. It was Mandy with a hand luggage all excited. I was in Anthony's shirt with my hair all messed up as we just got out of bed not long ago.

"You're just getting up?" Asked Mandy.

"The car is coming to pick us up in an hour," she said putting her bag down.

Anthony came in from the bathroom with just his towel around his waist, "Hello Mandy," he said.

"Well, hello, big boy!" Mandy purred looking at him lusciously.

"Alright. You can put him down now," I said walking over to Anthony and running my hand down his six-pack.

"Go get some clothes on, baby."

"Don't mind me," said Mandy still feasting on his body smiling at him.

He smiled back shaking his head at her harmless and outrageous flirtation and went off to the bedroom to change.

"You are such a bad girl," I said teasing her.

"Never mind that; you need to jump in the shower quick. I bet you didn't text Anthony's address to Joanne," she said.

Giving her a blank expression she huffed, "I knew you would forget so I sent it. I also brought some clothes and shoes for us to try on and choose which one to wear. Ooh, I'm so excited; I mean, the girl is mega rich. Did you see the way she was ordering that bottle of Canuti Champagne? They are like £200 a bottle. She even has her own driver. Oh! Boy, lucky girl," she said even more excited.

"Don't be excited about these things; money is not everything," I said unimpressed.

I went to shower while Mandy sort through the clothes to see which one to wear. When I came out from the bathroom, her makeup and hair was done. She helped me blow dry and tonged my hair. Anthony would not go; he said it was not his kind of thing. We were just about ready when the doorbell rang. Mandy squealed all excited, "How do I look?" she asked Anthony posing for him.

He gave her the thumbs up. She curtseyed towards him then ran to answer the door. I kissed Anthony and told him I would call him and fill him in about the party. I also asked him if he could drop off our stuff at Mandy's in the morning. With a final kiss, he admired the black sexy dress I was wearing.

"Be good," he said.

"I can't promise that," I replied, keeping him on his toes then we left.

Joanne's house was a huge mansion in Hampstead; a seven-bedroom house, indoor swimming pool with gold-plated mosaic tiles, a gym, spa, and sauna which Joanne could not wait to show us. Everything about her house was huge: the garden was lit up with fairy lights, the dining hall was wonderfully decorated with Christmas decorations. She took us to her room which was pink and very girlie almost like something out of a fairy tale. Mandy's jaw was opened throughout the tour of the house. Joanne brought us earlier than the rest of the guests because she wanted to show us around. She even offered us some of her designer clothes she'd never worn; they still had the price tags on them. Mandy and I were shocked to see how much the clothes cost. I declined and thanked her for her generosity though Mandy wanted the clothes.

I wondered what her dad did for a living. He was a property developer; she said later. She had so many things I didn't think was possible for one person to own so much. We stayed upstairs in her room for a while listening to music until her mom called us to come and join the party. Mandy and I had never seen so much food in our life; the champagne was flowing like water. They had an army of waiters and servants everywhere. The best part of the party was the fireworks in the garden. Though it was cold outside, it was really nice. I didn't want to stay too long at the party because I wanted a clear head in the morning to sort out my course work. But Mandy didn't want to go and Joanne wanted us to stay. I had little choice then! So we stayed until 11.30 pm when the driver took us home. The driver dropped me home first, then Mandy. When I got in, my foster sister was fast asleep; thank God! She is a nasty piece of work.

I spoke to Anthony briefly before going to sleep. I told him all about the party and how big Joanne's house was and everything. After saying goodnight, I went to bed thinking about him. As I was dropping off to sleep, I heard the door open then quickly closed again. It must have been Mr. Abbott checking up on us.

I was rudely woken up first thing in the morning by Francesca who was way overdue to move out. She had found a place and would move out in no time. She was nearly two years older than me and a big bully. She was what they would call a problem teenager with drug addiction. It was quite sad, really, because she was a pretty dark-skinned girl from the West Indies with lots of potential. I remember when I first moved in, thirteen then, she was so horrible. One night when she was high on drugs, she pinned me down on the bed and held a knife to my face and threatened me.

"You think you're so special, don't you? With your pretty hair and your pretty face and big smile always trying to help around the house, well you're not! I am Mr. Abbott's special girl, not you," she said angrily.

I was so scared she was going to kill me if I moved a muscle. I could feel the cold blade against my skin.

"I will slice your face and you won't look so pretty anymore. What do you think about that?" she said with a sinister laughter.

Out of the blue, Mr. Abbott came bursting in our room making her jump off me rapidly. She hid the knife behind her.

"What do you think you are doing, Francesca? He asked alarmingly. "Nothing. We were just messing," she replied laughing whilst dropping the knife on the ground.

"Get out!" he said sternly.

Francesca left the room feeling let down by him as he closed the door behind her. He came to the bed where I sat terrified and gave me a hug rubbing my back trying to comfort me but then he started to make me feel uncomfortable. I tried to pull away but he just held me there and started to smell my hair and rub his nose on my neck saying, "I will protect you. Don't be afraid. I will not let anything happen to you. You are my special girl."

I pushed him away forcefully fearing him more than Francesca a moment ago. I told him I was much better and just wanted to go out and get some fresh air. From that day on I became very wary of him and made sure I was never left alone with him.

I sat up on my bed annoyed why Francesca would wake me up that early on a Sunday morning. Still, I was determined not to let her get to me that New Year; not to mention she would leave soon.

"I thought you said you would stay at Mandy's the whole weekend; what you doing here?" she asked in her usual rude manner.

"Not that is any of your business but I want to get a head start with some of my coursework," I replied rubbing my eyes to wake up.

"You're already a brainy box, can't you even relax and enjoy your Christmas holidays? I'm sure that boyfriend of yours will be happy to spend time with you," she said smiling.

"Shhh! Keep your voice down," I whispered.

"What? You're afraid they will find out that their little Miss Perfect is screwing around," she mocked.

"I am not screwing around and you better not say anything about Anthony to them," I said, before she cut me off abruptly.

"Or what?" she said acutely.

"Aaarrgh, fine I will go and leave you alone," I said in frustration jumping out of bed.

I had my bath, skipped breakfast and gathered the coursework I needed. I packed some clothes and was on my way out when I heard Mr. Abbott and Francesca whispering in the kitchen. I listened in wondering if she was telling him about me and Anthony. I wished I hadn't because what I heard was very disturbing. I found out Mr. Abbott and Francesca were sleeping together. Sickened by what I had heard, I ran out of the door slamming it shut behind me. I couldn't believe it. How could he do that? How could she let him touch her? I knew he was a dirty sleazy old man but I didn't think he could go that far. Then, I knew why she was eager to get rid of me and why he allowed me to spend all the time I wanted away from home. How sordid! He must be the one giving her all the money to buy her drugs. I contemplated on what to do; whether or not to inform Mrs. Abbott.

When I got to Mandy's, she was still sleeping. As I waited, Mrs. Gray made me breakfast. After eating I went to do some of my coursework. Mandy woke up around midday surprised to see me at her place. By the time she finished getting ready and eating, I had advanced with my work and was ready for a break. Just then the doorbell rang; it was Anthony who was not expecting to see me there. After Anthony dropped off Mandy's hand luggage, Mandy and I decided to go to the pub. Anthony came, too. I got us a round of drinks although Anthony was on an orange juice. They could see I was troubled about something so I started to tell them everything that happened earlier in the morning at mine. Anthony was shocked and became angry and fearful for my safety. Up until then, I had never really discussed my home life or upbringing with him. Mandy told him how Mr. Abbott constantly tried to sleazy on me and how he tried it on her when she was once at mine. It began to dawn on me that when Francesca moved out, I would be left alone in my room and he could come in at any time. With some trepidation, I picked up my vodka and lemonade and drank it like water. Anthony and Mandy looked at me with concern. Anthony asked if I was alright; I said I wanted another drink, double straight with no ice. Mandy went to buy the drinks then Anthony turned to me and looking disturbed, "What is it?" He asked, "…and don't say nothing because I know something is wrong. You don't have to do it tough all the time you know. I'm here for you," he said holding my hand.

"Francesca has gotten her flat. She will leave anytime from now and I will be left alone in the room, what if….?" I began to ask but unable to finish the sentence because I was afraid to even think about what Mr. Abbott could do to me.

Anthony shifted his chair closer to mine and held my shoulders, turning me to face him as he looked into my eyes, "There is no way I am going to let that monster lay his filthy hands on you," he said firmly. "That's it! You are moving in with me and never going back to that house again. Why don't you report him so he won't be able to do this to someone else again?

How can the authorities allow someone like him to foster kids? It makes me sick just thinking about it."

"What did I miss?" asked Mandy in her usual quirky way returning with our drinks.

"Sandra is moving in with me!" declared Anthony.

"No, I'm not," I said raising my voice with a little annoyance.

I took my drink and knocked it back and asked Anthony to buy a round of tequilas for us. Reluctantly, he did. Mandy and I got drunk and we were the last people to leave the pub at closing. Anthony dropped Mandy home then I spent the night at his. When I woke up late morning, Anthony was out. I saw a note he left saying he had been called in to work. I lazed around the house bored. I called Mandy to come round. She came with Joanne. They giggled as they arrived. I opened the door only to find they both had two bottles of champagne in their hands. "The cavalry has arrived!" said Mandy giggling as she entered followed by Joanne.

It seemed that they both started to drink before they came over; I had some catching up to do. We finished the four bottles of champagne and realised we were hungry. Joanne took us to some posh Italian restaurant. We had a great time; the waiters were chatting us up and one of them gave me his number. Joanne ordered so much food that I took some home for Anthony as I knew he would be very hungry after his long shift at the hospital. I wanted to be home around nine which would be the time he would be back from work. After dinner, Joanne's driver dropped me at Anthony's. The girls wanted to come in as it was still early. In no time, they wanted to go to a night club. I wanted to go too but I knew Anthony would be too tired. They insisted that I should let my hair down and stop being an old woman and pushed their way in. Anthony just came out of the shower, and we were quite very jovial and loud as teenagers often are but I felt slightly bad because he was quite tired. I served the food for Anthony. After eating, he went to bed because he had an early shift in the morning. We got ready and went to the club. I didn't go back to Anthony's because I didn't want to disturb him so we ended up at Joanne's which pleased Mandy a great deal. Since it was only a couple of days left before school, I was in a rush to get back home. Even though Joanne played the perfect host to both of us, we swam in her beautiful swimming pool and spent a long time in the spa. We had a go at everything; the gym, sauna and Jacuzzi. Her waiters were also at our beck and call. We were waited on hand and foot; it was like being on a holiday on a private island. That was exactly what I needed after all the boozing and stress of home life. I could go back to school rejuvenated and ready to throw myself into my studies and ace my final-year ready for university in September.

I wanted to spend a nice quiet time with Anthony before I went back home because I knew I would not have much time for him until after my final exams near summer then I would be off to university.

It's been over a month Anthony and I have not seen each other though we text and speak on the phone as often as we could. My mind was primarily on my course work. He was also busy with work. Valentine's Day arrived and he wanted us to spend some time together. He was so happy to see me and as lovely as it was to see him, my mind was with the work I had to do.

"Sandra, can't you switch off for just a few hours?" He asked disappointingly, "I haven't seen you in such a long time and besides you are going to ace your exams. I have never seen anyone as laborious as you. You will be off to university soon and I don't know when I will see you again. Please, babe, let's enjoy the time we have and make the most of it."

I began to feel bad seeing all the effort he put into preparing me a romantic meal, the wine with flowers and everything. I kissed him and apologised and we had a wonderful evening.

Liberated

Francesca moved out finally at the end of February. There was a look of relief in her eyes as she left. I almost felt pity for her trying to imagine what she must have gone through. The room felt strange with just me there. Funny enough, I missed not having her there. The first two nights, I was apprehensive about Mr. Abbott trying to sneak into the room. I did not sleep too well. After a week of being on the alert and nothing happening, I let my guard down; I should have known better. My eyes were heavy with sleep one night; I spent most of my time in the library when I got home I just crashed. I thought I heard the door to my bedroom open but I was too tired to look. Not long after that, I felt a hand touch my leg. I froze knowing who it was. I was too scared to move hoping he would go away but he didn't. Lucky for me, I heard Mrs. Abbott call out.

"Is that you, Donald? Can I have a glass of water, too, dear?" He moved his hand quickly as if he just got an electric shock from my leg and left my room closing the door gently. I let out a huge sigh of relief but I could not sleep for the rest of the night. The next morning, I left without breakfast and was highly stressed out. After school, I went to Mandy's and told her what happened. She wanted me to inform Anthony but I objected because he could do something crazy to Mr. Abbott and insist I moved in with him. I sought Mrs. Abbott's permission to be at Mandy's for a while.

Friday evening, Mr. Abbott called me and said that he and Mrs. Abbott were going to the Lakes for the weekend and needed someone to be in the house and that I should come home since they were leaving first thing in the morning. I called Mrs. Abbott to be sure they were really going before I went home. She confirmed it was so. I went back midday when I was sure that they were gone. I called Anthony and told him I had the house to myself for the whole weekend. It was going to be the perfect opportunity to see my place. I promised to cook him dinner. After dinner, we began talking about my foster parents and Francesca wondering how she was doing. As far as I knew, she had not called since she moved out.

Not long after we went up to my room did we hear the front door open. I signalled Anthony to hide in the closet and I turned off the light and laid down on my bed pretending to be asleep. I heard my bedroom door open. Mr. Abbott called my name but I ignored him. He called the second time saying he knew that I was not asleep because he saw the light on. I sat up on the bed covering my body with the duvet. He told me not to be frightened and that he just wanted to apologise for making me feel uncomfortable and things were going to change for the better from then on.

Unsure whether to believe him or not, I asked where Mrs. Abbott was, and he told me she was still at the Lakes, that he told her he was feeling poorly so he had to come home and insisted that she should stay and enjoy herself with her friends. My radar shot up! He put his hands on my shoulders and moved closer.

"It's just you and me in the house. You cannot elude me this time. I have waited for this moment for years," he said.

I cringed in repugnance.

"Oh! Don't look like that... it's not like we are blood-related and you seem to like older men so I don't see what the problem is. I know you have been giving it away to that... that Anthony guy all this while denying me what is rightfully mine," he continued.

I could see that something was seriously not right about this man as I looked on in disgust.

"Oh! Yes, good old Francesca told me all about it. And there I was thinking you were pure and innocent waiting to be plucked."

"You are sick, Mr. Abbott. You need help," I said, trying to pull away from him but he tightened his grip.

"You are a very beautiful woman," he said stroking my face lustfully.

"I am a girl, not a woman," I said recoiling away. He laughed sickly.

"I bet that Anthony guy will disagree with you when he is giving it to you rough and hard huh.... now come here," he demanded pinning me down and forcefully trying to kiss me.

55

Before I knew it, Anthony flew out of my wardrobe irate and threw him off me then pounced on Mr. Abbott punching and kicking him. I screamed for Anthony to stop as I tried to pull him off telling him that he was not worth it. Mrs. Abbott burst into the room and commanded Anthony to get off him. We all watched Mr. Abbott down on the floor with his bloody face. It was an ignominious end to the years of abuse. We all left him there and followed Mrs. Abbott downstairs to the sitting room where she poured all of us a glass of rum. She knocked hers back and poured another. I was still shaking at what had happened. I wanted to talk about it but Anthony was still fuming. As for Mrs. Abbott, she was overly cool about what she witnessed.

"Don't you want to know what happened?" I asked walking over to her.

She took a deep breath, sighed and knocked her drink back again straightening herself up.

"I don't need to know," she replied.

"What?" I said shocked by her reaction.

She could not look at me. I glanced over at Anthony who was puzzled so I pressed on, "He tried to…."

"I said I don't want to know!" She screamed at me hysterically.

Astounded, I went over to Anthony who put his arms around me. He too was disturbed by her outburst. Composing herself, she walked over to me regretful and said sorry, then it dawned on me that she knew. She knew about his abuse to Francesca and who knows how long he had been abusing children under their care. Appalled that she knew all those years and did nothing, I could do nothing but cry. I felt so betrayed by the ones that were supposed to protect me. I thought she loved me; how wrong I was! I looked over at Anthony who told me to pack my things that I would not stay in that mad house. I went up and packed all my things and left and never looked back.

It was the last week of my final exams. I had been working flat out waking up early and sleeping late; sometimes forgetting to eat if Anthony didn't remind me. He was super supportive; I don't know what I would have done without him. My eighteenth birthday and our first year anniversary of being together was approaching but the only thing I could think about was finishing my exams and making sure I got top marks. Since I moved in Anthony's, I wasn't seeing Mandy as much as before unless in school. I had not seen Joanne in months though she called and wanted to go out clubbing. Sometimes I wondered if she ever studied.

Exams were all over after fourteen gruesome days. I could then sleep for a week if I wished. For the anniversary, I cooked a lovely meal for Anthony and me. I didn't really have much money to buy him a present. However, Anthony came home with a big bouquet of red roses.

"Mmm, something smells nice," said Anthony.

I came out of the kitchen walking over to him seductively in my black and red baby doll lingerie and chemises with my black stilettos.

"But the view is even better," he said delightfully as he dropped the things on the table speedily grabbing and kissing me passionately. We made love right there and then as passion swooped over us; that must have been the most passionate urge I had ever seen in him.

We celebrated my birthday next. Joanne turned up first thing in the morning surprisingly to take me to a luxurious spa. She took me to get my hair, nails, and make-up done. I was treated like a princess. It was a beautiful day and I wished Mandy could've come along. She would have loved it. We went from the spa to Joanne's and had something to eat. After, she presented me with boxes and a bag of presents beautifully wrapped. I looked at her inquisitively; she motioned for me to open them, more excited than me.

I was a little uncomfortable to open the gifts as I felt she had done more than enough. I knew she had spent a lot of money on me already. She wanted me to open the bag of Chanel first; so I did. There was a beautiful, yellow, one-shoulder short dress with an over-the-shoulder strap with bow ornamentation. The waistband had a beaded broach and a wire hem. She asked me to try it on; it was a perfect fit. She handed over another box for me to open; it was a white heel sandal from Diane von Furstenberg. She nodded for me to put them on and I did. In the next box was a white handbag from Luella. I looked in the mirror and did a twirl. She came over with the final box which was the smallest.

"This will complete the outfit; you can't dress without accessorising," she said smiling.

I opened it and gasped; it was a diamond necklace and matching teardrop earrings from Graff. I looked at her, shaking my head in amazement that she would spend so much on me.

"I can't accept this. You have done more than I could ever imagine in this world," I said handing it back to her.

She would not hear of it and insisted I kept them. She told

me not to look at the price and that it was pocket change for her. She took out the necklace and put it on me.

"See!" She said, "It looks great on you; put the earrings on," she insisted clapping her hands eagerly.

"You should keep up with the modelling. You look fab! I can see why you get all the blokes. If I was a bloke, I would definitely be into you," she said jokingly.

"Shut up!" I said giving her a little shove and we both started laughing. I turned to face her looking all serious.

"You know you don't have to buy my friendship, Joanne. You're a nice person and I am happy to call you my friend. I know we haven't been spending that much time together but that's just because of my exams. When it comes to working hard, I tend to shut everyone out to get on with it. It's nothing personal."

"Yeah I know," she said continuing, "That's what makes me want to buy you nice things because I know you are genuinely my friend not just because I'm rich unlike so many of my other so-called friends. You're real and everyone loves you for being you and I can be myself around you. I don't have to pretend and you couldn't care less about money."

"Oh! I wouldn't go that far," I said and we both burst out laughing.

I gave her a big hug and thanked her for everything; I had such a wonderful day and I still had the night to look forward to. Joanne said she was meeting up with some friends for a drink before the night club later so she got changed. Anthony planned on taking me out to dinner to meet the girls later in a club so the outfit was perfect. Joanne's chauffeur opened the door for us to enter the black limousine stretched out in front of the mansion. I couldn't believe it. When we arrived at mine, she said she wanted to come in and say hello to Anthony. While she made a quick call I went ahead to open the door to a massive shout of 'surprise!' with everyone jumping out from different directions. I nearly jumped out of my skin.

I looked at Joanne behind me who smiled broadly then Mandy came rushing towards me and gave me a big hug and a kiss wishing me a happy birthday. Anthony came forward and moved Mandy away saying it was his turn facetiously. He held out my hands looking me over admiringly; he gave me a big birthday kiss then walked me over to the center. The party went on until the early hours of the morning. The place was jam-packed with our friends since it was also Mandy's party.

Everyone had a good time. Some of Anthony's colleagues from work came, too. He introduced me to Tracey, the nurse, whom he worked with; she was nice and a bit older than me. There was so much food and drinks. I was so filled with joy that I lost my appetite. I had never felt so happy. I wanted the moment to last forever. Anthony had gone through so much trouble to throw me this surprise party with the help of Joanne and Mandy; I was really touched by the gesture.

The summer was going to be the last before I went to Oxford University. Mandy didn't get in so she was going to Manchester University which put a damper on our holiday though Joanne tried to make sure we saw the positive side of it. We partied and clubbed a lot. I made sure I spent as much time with Anthony as

I could. Joanne taught me everything she knew about designer clothes. I couldn't believe she could tell the difference between a fake and genuine Fendi bag from a mile off. I began developing a taste for designer clothes so I took on a lot of modelling jobs. The more I did, the more in demand I became. I was earning big money; enough to get my own place but Anthony didn't want me to move out since I was moving to university; it would be a waste of money, he reasoned.

Finally, summer was over and it was time for a new chapter of my life. I was so excited but sad for leaving Anthony. The last two days before going off to university was difficult. He was so solemn; each night when we went to bed, he would hold me so tight before he slept. He was afraid to let go as if he was never going to see me again. I tried to reassure him that nothing was going to change and that I was going to visit as often as I could.

"Nothing ever stays the same, babe," he argued.

I looked at the heart locket he got me for my birthday with the inscription: *Forever yours, Anthony.* I rubbed it, then kissed his shoulder and went to sleep.

Chapter Five

The Unexpected

"I am pregnant!" I sobbed down the phone to Mandy.

"What?" She yelled shocked.

"Are you sure?" she asked.

I looked out the window; the rain was coming down so hard I thought the heavens were crying with me. I sat down on my bed and thanked God that my roommate was not there. She was so nosy and loved to gossip. If she even got a whiff that I was pregnant, not only would Oxford but the whole of Cambridge University will know about it. Mandy asked me if I had told Anthony; I said no. I didn't know how to tell him and I didn't know what to do. It's only been two months I'd been here and just settled in. How could I have been so stupid? We had always been so careful. I couldn't think clearly.

Mandy urged me to call Anthony to tell him; so I did. He was quiet at first, then he asked me if I was sure. I told him I had not seen my period for two months and I was always regular. He then asked if I had seen a doctor. I told him I hadn't yet. I started to cry again but he insisted on coming up to Oxford. I told him not to bother and that I would come down to London for the weekend. I had a photoshoot for a magazine cover. We spoke for a while longer and was saying our goodbyes when my roommate came in. The rest of the week seemed to drag on forever. Anthony and Mandy called almost every minute to check up on me. I knew they cared about me but it started to get on my nerves after a while; causing me to snap at them a couple of times.

The photoshoot was first thing on Saturday morning. They put us in a hotel on Friday night to ensure we were well rested and on schedule. I went straight to the hotel from the train station. I couldn't face Anthony and I didn't want to think about anything other than the photoshoot. I called him to let him know I had arrived in London but I would stay at the hotel and I would see him after the shoot. There were three of us doing the modelling; one I had worked with before but the other I hadn't; she was very frosty. The shoot was monotonous and long. I called Anthony as soon as we were done to inform him I was on my way.

When I got home, he was all spruced up wearing my favorite cologne that I bought him for his birthday which I could smell as he approached to kiss me. He took my bag and sat me down, took off my shoes and put my feet up on the stool. I didn't say a word. I just watched him act nervously as if I was an invalid. He made us a romantic meal but he hardly touched his food. I asked for wine but he told me it wasn't a good idea in my condition.

He started to bubble on like he does when he was really nervous. Then finally, he went on one knee and asked me to marry him. I was stunned by his proposal. I couldn't say anything. I turned away and he got up feeling dejected. I got up from the dinner table and sat down on the sofa. How could I marry him? I just turned eighteen. I had my education to finish and I had my career ahead. My worst nightmare seemed to be coming true. When I was in foster care, there were so many teenage pregnancies; girls that had their lives ruined and dropped out of school at fourteen…fifteen. I was determined not to be one of them.

I started to cry feeling sorry for myself; he came over and held me as he apologized. He told me that he loved me and wanted to have children with me. He was only waiting until I finished university before he proposed but he was very happy that I was having his baby. Nevertheless, he didn't want to pressure me if I didn't want to get married. I began to cry again because he was being so nice about the whole thing. I told him I wasn't ready to be a mom or to settle down. He let go of me and asked what I meant by not being "ready to be a mom" with a look of horror on his face; I knew what he was thinking.

I also knew he had a strong religious belief. I told him I had worked too hard to throw it all away. I wasn't sure what I wanted to do next. I needed more time to think things through. Just then, there was a knock at the door. We both got up from the sofa. I stood in the hallway while he went to open the door. It was his parents, Janet and Robert. His mom came in with a big brown teddy bear with a pink ribbon on the neck. She bypassed Anthony and walked straight to me stretching out her hands to embrace me.

"Ooh! My beautiful daughter! You have given me a grandchild at last; you have made me so happy," she said in her African accent kissing my cheek.

"Congratulations both wit da engagement an-da baby, you no mi-a proud- a-you," his father said in his strong Jamaican accent.

I was gob smacked by what I was hearing. All I could do was run to the bedroom and shut the door. After a while, Anthony came in and sat on the bed. He rubbed my back as I lay there on the bed looking away from him. He apologized for his mom and dad and told me that they had left. He asked for my forgiveness explaining that he got carried away when he found out I was pregnant and mentioned it to his dad who then informed his mom. I told him I wanted an early night because I wanted to follow him to go to church in the morning which was a surprise and also a delight to him because he had tried many times to invite me to church but I turned down his invitations. Not really because I did not want to go to church, but rather that I always came back late from a night club or had a terrible hangover. It was always one thing or the other.

Somehow on that particular day, I felt by going to church with Anthony, perhaps, just perhaps, I might find the answers to my predicament. After all, I was a Christian although not a practising one; I attributed my predicaments to the absence of God in my life. I needed to take God and the things of God seriously if only He could help me out of the situation, I thought. For the first time in a very long time, I prayed to God to forgive and help me. I promised to become a faithful Christian from then on. After praying, I felt at peace then fell asleep. That night was the first night Anthony and I did not hold each other while sleeping. We slept backing each other.

We went to church the following morning. It wasn't what I was expecting. I thought it was going to be boring but it was quite lively. I saw Anthony's friend, Tracey; she was so friendly. We spoke for a short while then we exchanged numbers. Anthony's mom and dad were in church, too. They apologized about the night and said that they loved me and hoped to see me soon. My head was a little clearer but I was still a bit scared. I was having stomach cramps, perhaps, from not having any breakfast; not to mentions all the stress.

We did not hang around for long after the service. He took me home to rest. When we got home, he tried so hard to be nice. He gently sat me down on the sofa, took off my shoes and went to make me something to eat. He was such a lovely man, so thoughtful and kind. If only I was much older, I would gladly marry him and have his baby in a heartbeat but not then. Later on that evening, I found out my menstruation had started. I was so relieved and ecstatic. I thanked God and rushed over to Anthony. I gave him a big hug and told him the news. His facial expression changed and he looked sad though he tried to mask it. I was so happy and relieved I didn't stop to think of how he felt. The journey back to school was quiet. He did not utter a word throughout. I kissed him goodbye when we got there. From that moment, I knew things had changed between us.

I called Mandy as soon as I could to tell her the good news. We both screamed on the phone overjoyed. She asked me how everything went with Anthony. I filled her in the whole weekend.

Months passed and there seemed to be a growing distance between Anthony and me. We spoke less and less and also my visit home depleted. As a final point, I met some boy from uni and we started seeing each other; at first, we were just friends. He also taught me to drive. For my nineteenth birthday, he bought me a brand new incredibly luxurious sports car; a fountain blue metallic 2010 Bentley Continental GTC Convertible. Up until that moment, we have not been intimate but that night, to my shame, we ended up sleeping together.

I knew Abdul was a bit of a charmer and a playboy who had been after me since I got there; he claimed that I was not like the other girls that he loved me. He's a foreign student from a wealthy family in Dubai; we spent the summer there. I took Mandy and Joanne along. I even asked Tracey if she would come though it was awkward she was Anthony's friend but she agreed. All expenses were paid. Abdul lavished me with extravagant gifts including a penthouse apartment situated in prestigious Knightsbridge Garden Square.

The property had recently been refurbished to tip-top condition and had the benefit of a large roof terrace and reception room that offered spectacular triple aspect views over London. It had three double-bedrooms with three en suite bathrooms, a reception room, kitchen/breakfast room, a large roof terrace, a loft, resident porterage, a use of communal square garden's and a garage parking. When he handed over the key and the deeds for the flat with my name on it; it felt as though I was dreaming. We had not been together for that long but I already had a car and a flat worth millions of pounds; not to mention all the jewelry. I couldn't believe how much my life had changed in just a year.

I sent a Gucci watch to Anthony for his birthday but he returned it unopened. I wanted to call him but I didn't know what to say. He was not too thrilled when he found out I was seeing Abdul. I was frequently in London when I did not have any lecture or modelling assignments. My face seemed to be popping up everywhere. I was even offered to be the face of L'Oreal. I was on top of the world and I just wished Anthony was happy and could move on. I wanted us to remain friends. My modelling career had really taken off. My agent wanted me to leave school and go full-time but I wanted to get my degree and have something to fall back on. There was a big party in London. All the usual celebrities would be there; of course, as always, I invited the girls. Abdul went ahead to London on Thursday. We agreed to meet Saturday night at the party. I informed him I would be in London on Saturday about noon. However, I finished up with what I had to do so I decided to go home on Friday instead to surprise him.

Whenever Abdul was in London, he stayed with me even though he had his own place in Hyde Park. When I got in, I could hear two giggling from my bedroom. I had a very bad feeling and thought for a moment about not going in but I had to see for myself. I went in only to find Abdul in bed with some blondy.

"Don't let me interrupt," I said putting on a brave front.

I walked over to my wardrobe and took out a dress to go clubbing. As I was leaving the room I heard her ask him who I was. He snapped at her and told her to get dressed and get out while he hurriedly dressed. Half-dressed, he ran after me and apologizing. I didn't want to hear anything he had to say and that was the last I saw of him other than in the university from time to time. That night, I turned up at Anthony's crying my eyes out; he comforted me and we ended up sleeping together. We also went to the celebrity party on Saturday. The girls were surprised to see us back together. I explained to them what happened and we went on to enjoy the night. After the party, he came back to my flat and stayed the night. It was the first time he had seen my place. He was impressed and stated jokingly that at least I got the biggest pay-out for dating Abdul for six months.

Things between Anthony and I were not the same. I knew that my feelings for him had changed. The passion was not there anymore. Not long after we got back together, I strayed again and started to date a footballer I met in a nightclub. That also fizzled out after a couple of months when his friend made a play for me. I dated a couple of male models; big mistake! Never date anyone who spends more time admiring himself in the mirror than you; I seem to drift from one disastrous relationship to the next. It was either I was the trophy girlfriend or they cheated on me, became too possessive or controlling. One of them tried to get me to start taking cocaine and told me it was the celebrity culture and that everyone was doing it. One of the footballers I dated after drinking heavily one night slapped my face in a jealous rage when a man wanted my autograph. He accused me of flirting and leading him on. I was fed up with the grievous relationships I kept getting myself into. So I went back to Anthony once again. I was surprised that he took me back.

Things were going well between Anthony and me for a while, my modelling career was going great, university was fine but my private life was unsatisfactory. Somehow, then I met Steve. It wasn't an instant attraction as he really was not my type. He pursued me for a while before I finally gave in since the ones that had been my type hadn't worked out. He was funny and sweet, not overly good-looking. He had blond hair and blue eyes. He was so humble. He wasn't from a rich family. He worked hard to pay his way in the university. Sometimes, he would struggle to make ends meet but he would be too proud to let me help him. It would take great persuasion before he would accept what he called, "a handout" from me. I liked the fact that he didn't treat me like a celebrity or see me as a rich person. It felt like when I was in my early teens again.

We went out for five months and it seemed things were going so well. He never failed to tell me how much he loved me every day. He loved spending time in my flat in London so we went there as often as we could until one day when I was coming to his student house, I overheard him and his friends talking about me and how he had won the bet to sleep with me. I heard him say that I was just a rich bitch with more money than sense then all of them started laughing. One of them added that I was in the right profession that all models were dumb heads. He went on to say that I probably slept my way to university and all I had to do was flutter my eyelashes at the lecturers and they would give me good marks, he mocked. I was shocked that he had me fooled. I was angry with myself for being fooled. Determined that they would not have the last laugh, I quickly composed myself and knocked at the door. I went in all sweet and bubbly as if I had heard nothing. I greeted them as always and kissed Steve passionately leaving him with a kiss he would not forget in a hurry as his friends looked on. One of them called out to get a room. I stopped and pulled away, "Sorry, boys," I said, "It's just that Steve is such a nice boy I can't help myself, in fact, all of you have been so nice to me so I decided to treat you all to VIP tickets to the Arsenal v Manchester game this weekend."

They jumped up with excitement and said I was the best. One of his friends said that they did not know I was this nice almost with regret. I left closing the door behind me and listened at the door. I heard them chattering in excitement; one of them said to Steve that he should hold on to me that I was worth my weight in gold. I snorted and headed off inflamed. Friday could not come fast enough for Steve and his friends. They were so hyped up about the game; I gave them the instructions that when they got to Emirates Stadium, the tickets were under Steve's name reserved by one of the footballers I knew, and that they would be taken inside to meet the players after. I went back to London to Anthony's but met his absence. I went to his workplace at the hospital. I saw Tracey who told me where he was so I went there and found him and one of the nurses kissing. I tried to leave but he spotted me and stopped as if doing something he was not supposed to and ran after me. I was a bit jealous though I had no right to be; it's just that in all the years I had known him, I had never ever seen him with anyone else other than me. I suppose he must have been with other women when we were not together but I have never seen them. I ran off crying stupidly. He caught up with me and comforted me. I kissed him as if to prove a point or just to make sure he still loved me. I could not tell but it was not a smart move. The nurse he was kissing stormed off; I guess she must have seen us kissing. I felt bad for her but all I could think about then was how unhappy I was. Anthony said his shift would be finished in a couple of hours. I told him to come over to mine after work and I would cook him a nice meal.

On my way out, I heard the nurse he was kissing earlier complaining to some of the other nurses about me. "Who does she think she is? Just because she's a top model doesn't give her the right to come over like that and kiss my boyfriend," she said. "I don't even know what he sees in her, anyway."

"Err, she's hot! She is rich, famous and gorgeous; a perfect figure…need I go on? She is every man's dream," a colleague of hers said.

Tracey was working behind the nurses' station and told them to get back to work and stop gossiping. She turned to the girl Anthony was kissing and reminded her that she warned her not to get involved with Anthony because he was still in love with me. When Anthony's girlfriend saw me coming, she gave me a dirty look but did not say a word. I pretended I did not see her and walked straight over to Tracey. I spoke to her briefly and left.

When Anthony came to my flat, I had the place lit up with candles, a romantic table set out and I cooked his favorite meal. I wore my Shirley of Hollywood Babydoll lingerie with embellished molded underwired padded push-up cups, romantic flounces down the skirt, stretch net back with G-string. When he knocked, I opened the door seductively and his jaw dropped as he fixated his eyes on my breasts, then his eyes slowly travelled up and down my body. I pulled him in towards me, "You like?" I asked.

"Me like," he replied slowly with satisfaction.

He started to kiss me hungrily as he directed me to my bedroom while still kissing; he whispered in my ear between kisses how he had missed me. After making love, we showered and ate. We held each other while sitting on the sofa and watching television in silence. I did not need to say anything about what happened as he already knew that things had gone wrong with Steve. We spent the whole weekend together though I stopped over to see Joanne. I went back to Oxford after the weekend. Throughout Sunday afternoon until evening, my mobile phone won't stop ringing so I put it on silent mode. Anthony asked me if it was Steve; I told him it was but I had nothing more to say to him. In the end, I told him what Steve did and what he and his friends said about me. He was really angry about what they did and wished he could meet them and let them know what they did was wrong. I told him not to worry that I already got even with them without getting into details because I knew he would not approve as he did not believe in revenge due to his religious belief.

I often teased him about sleeping with me without being married and that it was biblically wrong and a sin. He would laugh and say, 'You are my only weak device and I would marry you in a heartbeat if you would let me'. I had a really nice weekend and I apologized to him about crashing his romance with his girlfriend. He told me she was not his girlfriend and that it was nothing serious. He further assured that there was only one girl in his life and that was me and always will be.

Steve came to my student house but I wasn't there. My roommate, Stella, told him I was in the library. He came looking for me in the library. He tried talking to me but we couldn't really talk there so I told him I would meet him later in his room. He left impatiently clinching his teeth. Before I went to his room, I took an envelope full of cash and one of the gold necklaces and a diamond bracelet Abdul bought for me worth over £50,000. When I got there, he didn't bother to kiss me. He got straight to the point.

"I have been phoning you since Saturday and you have not answered any of my calls. I came to your flat hoping to spend the night there before the game on Sunday but you were not there. My friends and I were disgraced and then thrown out by the security when we arrived at Emirates Stadium, there was no ticket reserved for us. We spent so much money coming down to London only to be humiliated like that," he said angrily.

"First of all you need to calm down. Secondly, my phone was stolen, and thirdly... my friends and I went out for drinks then on to a night club. How was I supposed to know you were trying to get hold of me? I thought you were too busy having fun with your friends?" I said defensively walking away from him acting all hurt.

He came over and gave me a hug apologizing. I pulled a face repulsed by his touch. He narrated all the things that happened at the stadium. I sympathized with him and encouraged him to get changed so that I could take him out to a posh meal to cheer him up. While he went to change, I planted the money and jewelry under his pillow. When we left his room, I told him that I wanted to change into something more appropriate and asked him to wait in the car as I would not be long. Once I was sure that I was out of his sight, I took out my mobile phone and called the police to report my items missing.

The police asked me who would have access to my room. I informed them that my roommate and Steve had access to my room. Within ten minutes, the police arrived as I was coming out. Steve saw them walking towards me and got out of my car. I motioned for him to come whilst I spoke to the police briefly. We all went back to my room and my roommate, Stella, was surprised to see me and Steve with the police. The policewoman took Stella to one side and had a word with her. I could see a shocked look on her face as she raised her arms in denial shaking her head. The policewoman joined her partner and they began to search Stella's things to her displeasure. I filled Steve in about my missing items and told him that the police may likely search his room too since he was my boyfriend and had access to my room. I assured him that the gesture was to eliminate him as a suspect from their enquiries. Steve was more than willing to assist and cooperate with the police. The police did not find anything in my roommate's belongings. They apologized to her and assured her that they were only doing their job, she was not too thrilled but understood. Next stop was Steve's. The police began to search his room as soon as Steve let us in. Steve was ultra-helpful to the police confident that they would not find anything in his room. When they discovered my items under his pillow, his face went pale; he could not believe what his eyes were seeing. Of course he denied knowing anything about them or how they got there. The police arrested him and took him away. As he got into the car, he looked at me helplessly and I gave him a devious smile to let him know that I set him up.

Stella, my roommate, rang the papers and told them everything. The next day, the national newspapers' head line was "Boyfriend Stole Thousands Worth of Jewelry and Cash from Supermodel Girlfriend" with a picture of me on the front cover. The paper had a picture of Steve in it and that of Anthony, too. The story in the paper was how I dumped Steve to go back to my long-time on-and-off boyfriend, Dr. Anthony Wilson, and how Steve stole from me as revenge. It went on to talk about my long string of failed relationships and how I always went back to Anthony. It finished off by saying that I should do fellows out there a favor and just marry Anthony instead of breaking men's heart and giving them false hope and then go running back to Dr. Wilson." That very morning when I came out of my room to go to the library, people kept staring at me more so than usual. I was unaware of the story in the paper until one of my classmates came with the paper and showed it to me. For a moment I wondered how the papers got the story so fast...

it was only Steve, Stella, and the police who knew about it. It suddenly occurred to me that Stella must have been the one to blab to the papers. I stormed off in search of her; I found her in the hall with her friends. In anger I threw the paper at her, "This is your hand work, isn't it?" I yelled. "Don't bother denying it because I already know it's you. You have no idea what you are talking about.... if you are going to kiss and tell at least make sure you got your facts right. Whatever amount of money they paid you, make sure you save it because you are going to need it for a lawyer. I am going to bring a defamation lawsuit against you, by the time you finish paying off your student loan and the lawyers you are going to wish you never crossed me." I left her there holding the paper terrified by what I had just said. I called Anthony to warn him about the paper but it was too late he had already seen it and was about to call me. I enlightened him to what I did to Steve and how my roommate sold the story to the papers. He was not happy that I set Steve up and insisted that I must go and tell the police the truth. He went on to ask why I didn't let him know what I was going to do beforehand. I explained to him that if I did, he would talk me out of it. Once I had agreed to go to the police, he laughed. "On a lighter note for once the papers are right about one thing: you should marry me and be done with it," he said light-heartedly.

Later on in the afternoon I called the police station and explained that it was all a misunderstanding that I remembered wearing the jewelry when we went out and when we were in bed together I must have taken it off so as not to break them and put it under his pillow but forget about it. Also, I brought the cash to give him to help pay for his student loan which I put under his pillow for him to find as a surprise. I apologized but they were not too happy for wasting their time. Not long after that, they released Steve and gave me back my things. Later that night, I went to Steve's and warned him that I never wanted to see or hear from him again and that if he crossed my path, he would regret it. I revealed to him that I heard everything he and his friends were discussing about me and how I was just a common bet for him to sleep with. After I finished revealing everything to him, he was furious and asked how I could set him and his friends up like that and have his face splashed in front of the newspapers. I told him that was not my doing but it was the hand work of my roommate. Notwithstanding, I was glad for that added bonus. "You are right bi…" He said angrily moving towards me like he was about to hit me. I cut him off backing away, "Ah, ah, ah, you don't want me to have you arrested for assault now, do you? You just got out; I mean I could have let you rot in jail and you could have kissed your precious education goodbye but I was kind enough to have your name cleared. As for the papers.… well, you have to take that one up with Stella," I said walking towards the door. I turned around and looked at him in disgust "I would have done anything for you and given you anything you wanted because I thought you were someone special; how wrong I was! Goodbye, Steve." I opened and slammed the door behind me.

Thank God it was the end of the term; I had Christmas holidays to look forward to and re-evaluate my life and what direction I wanted it to take. Stella had a run-in with Steve and she also attempted to apologize to me for her behavior but I was not interested so I just ignored her. After Stella found out what I did to Steve, she became terrified of what I would do to her. To put her out of her misery, I informed her that I would not go ahead with the lawsuit. That made her very relieved. I drove home for Christmas and excited to see the girls again because I hadn't seem Mandy for a while even though we spoke on phone all the time. I made up my mind to really have fun that Christmas holiday because after that, I would throw myself into my coursework as the next year would be my final year in uni. I went home, dropped my bags and went to Joanne's. She had a bottle of Santiago champagne chilling in the fridge though it was snowing and freezing outside. A cup of tea would have been more appropriate but you can't drink champagne warm; that would be preposterous. Anthony was on night duty so I didn't see him until late afternoon the following day. Mandy came back the day after I arrived. We all went out for a drink including Tracey but she didn't really drink much. We all had stories to tell of what happened since we all last saw one other; of course my appearance in the newspapers was the first topic to be brought up. I filled them in about the whole episode. We all giggled and laughed a lot. Mandy and Joanne applauded me for what I did but Tracey said she was just glad that I told the police the truth. Mandy said she was happy to see me and Anthony back together again, Joanne and Tracey nodded in unison with a happy grin on their faces.

"You should see him at work, you know... you could always tell when the two of you are back together, he's like a different person. His whole countenance changes; he comes alive," said Tracey. I smiled and she continued. "He is such a lovely man and you two belong together. You should put him out of his misery and just marry him. There are so many women out there throwing themselves at him but he only has eyes for you. There aren't many good guys out there, you know."

"Good guys are hard to find," said Joanne.

"What about your John?" I asked Tracey teasing her.

"Yes. Well, he's taken," she said all protective, and we all burst out laughing.

"I am not ready to get married," I said in a sober manner.

"I haven't even completed my education yet; I want to have fun first. Anthony is so serious, you know, I am afraid that marrying him would mean I would turn out to be a stay-at-home mom baking cookies and brownies and fat by the time I am thirty." I said and paused for a moment then continued, "I would probably end up marrying him but not now. I need to live first, and I don't know; perhaps, we met too early in life."

As the girls listened, I could see a sad expression on their faces but they understood. All in all, we had a great night. It was wonderful catching up with everyone. Tracey left early but we went on to a club and didn't come home until the early hours of the next morning. I met a couple of Italian guys who gave me their contacts but I didn't do anything as I promised myself to allow no distractions until I completed university.

The Christmas holidays seemed over before it began. We went to so many parties though Anthony and Tracey could not come to all because of their work. I threw a party at my flat too and, of course, Joanne's parents had their annual party. It was one of the best Christmas holidays I have had in a while. Things were also going well with Anthony and me or were it because of my determination not to stray. He seemed a bit more laid back too. I wondered if Tracey told him about our conversation about me marrying him; which would explain the change in his attitude.

Just after Christmas, I had a meeting with my agent, Marcy, to tell her that I did not want any more modelling assignments. I wanted to concentrate on my last year in university and I also informed her that when my contract with L'Oréal was up in the upcoming months, I was not going to renew it. She was not a happy woman. She said that I was making a very big mistake and that I was at the peak of my modelling career. Taking a year out was going to be a blow. Frankly, I didn't care; I had made up my mind that I didn't want to do modelling anymore. I wanted a profession in journalism or something in public relations. After what happened with Steve, I didn't want my private life splashed in front of the papers for people like Stella to feed on. Marcy was not happy with my decision but she respected it and said if I ever changed my mind, I should call her. We said our goodbyes.

Anthony and I had a lovely night together before I drove up to Oxford. I gave him a copy of the key to my flat to stay sometimes if he wanted; that made him happy because he loved staying at mine. I guess that also gave him hope about marriage between us. The New Year was a busy one; I kept to myself studying and when I needed a break, I would go down to London to see Anthony or he would drive up to see me with the new car I bought him for Christmas.

At long last, it was over. No more coursework, no more exams; what a relief! On the day of my graduation ceremony, Anthony and Joanne came. To my surprise, so did Mrs. Abbott, my foster mother. I wondered how she knew about my graduation. I had not set my eyes on her since the day I left. She seemed different, happier and at peace. I watched as she walked over nervously towards me and started crying. She apologized for not protecting me and all the other children from Mr. Abbott, then her ex-husband.

She said that she reported him to the authorities after I left; he was arrested and later sent to jail after conviction. She had been attending Anthony's church for over a year and begged Anthony to forgive her and to take her to my graduation. She told me she had made peace with God and wanted to make things right with me, too. Mrs. Abbott found Francesca and helped her come off drugs. She too had become a member of their church and she was doing well. I found it hard to believe; Francesca, a Christian. And she and Mrs. Abbott had become friends. I was happy she came off drugs.

I had a big party to celebrate the completion of my university education with excellent grades. I applied for a full-time job at the Canuti PR firm. It was the biggest such firm in London. I was certain that with my grades, I would be the status quo and get a job but they turned me down. I applied for several other positions but to no avail. I joined an agency to start off temping to gain some experience. I was also tempted to go back to modelling.

I even called Marcy to see if there was some work going. I did some temp jobs here and there until one day, I was offered a temp job working for the Canuti PR firm. Mandy still had to write her bar exams so I hang around with Joanne a lot. We partied and clubbed a lot which did not go down well with Anthony.

He seemed to be more religious and wanted us to get married now more than ever as I had completed university. I also noticed we have not slept together in a while. When I brought it up, he said he wanted to wait until we got married. Ever since he got baptized and became born-again, things changed between us. He didn't want to go to the nightclubs or the pubs with us anymore and he said that sleeping with me was fornication which is a sin and that he wanted to wait until we were married. I was not happy about that since we had been sleeping together for years and it never bothered him.

I accused him of using that to get me to marry him. We drifted apart eventually. I decided not to take men seriously anymore and just have them as a plaything. A relationship was not on the table any longer; just pure sex objects.

Chapter Six

Back to Reality

"She was murdered in her sleep," confided Mandy.

"What about her family?" I asked but she excused herself and put me on hold momentarily as another call was coming through. Meanwhile, my secretary entered with coffee and placed it on my desk; I thanked her and gave her the files of our new clients that needed urgent attention — working for one of the biggest public relations agencies in the city was never dull. My boss, Gianni, was out of the country on crisis management for one of our biggest clients and had left me in charge.

"Are you still there?" asked Mandy.

"Yeah," I replied.

"I have just reached their house and the security is tight, said Mandy. "The media is going to have a field day with this one," she continued.

"I'm sure you can handle it," I reassured her. "Besides, it's not like you haven't handled a high-profile case before though this is much bigger. They will make you a partner after this, I bet you. You know they are going to need PR services; don't forget to recommend us to them. It should please Gianni when he returns from his business trip."

"Amongst seeing your face, you mean," she said humorously.

"Very funny," I replied changing the subject, "Will you have time for lunch later? I want to find out how things are going with Aden," I drooled. Laughing on the other side of the phone, she said, "I will see what time I finish with my client then I will give you a ring, ciao Bella," taking a dig at Gianni.

"Bye," I said putting the phone down and taking a sip of my coffee.

I had some phone calls to make and a meeting to attend at midday; Annabel, my secretary, motioned from her desk to remind me — I could see her through my glass compartmented office. Annabel was a brilliant secretary; she knew what I wanted even before I asked her; highly efficient, organized and detail-oriented. She knew when to keep her mouth shut and when not to which was good because the mood of my colleagues at the office had turned increasingly belligerent as of last month after I got my promotion. Annabel didn't get involved with office politics; she kept her head down and got on with what she had to do. We seemed to be getting on well.

I went to the ladies to freshen up, came out and grabbed what I needed for the meeting which Annabel had left on my desk. She handed me a packet of mints; after thanking her, I popped a couple in my mouth to get rid of the coffee smell, put on my black sunglasses and left.

By 1:30 pm I was back in the office. As I walked in with my 4-inch micro black stiletto shoes with matching belt around my beautiful short white dress — all from Chanel; I could feel the glare of some of my work colleagues. Strutting past them I wriggled my butt ever the more. Annabel came over as I was about to enter my office in anticipation to find out how the meeting went. I gave her two thumbs up, she squealed giving a small clap. I turned around to face my work colleagues knowing that they were watching to see if I got the new contract or not. Seeing what I did, their faces were filled with indignation. I gave them an ingenious smile, opened my office door, went in, and closed it behind me.

I didn't have much time to dwell on how my colleagues felt about me before I saw all the messages on my desk especially the one from Gianni. I put my Chanel black bag on the table and the files from the meeting. Sitting down on my soft black leather chair behind my desk, I took off my sunglasses from my hair and ran my left fingers through it. I called Gianni at the hotel he was staying; they put me through to his room.

"Ciao Bella, come stai?" his voice rang out on the line.

"Hello Gianni, how are things over there….everything sorted? I asked with concern.

"Ah Bella, he sighed, things are a lot more complicated than they let us believe."

"Oh! I'm sure that there is nothing there you cannot handle," I said encouragingly.

"Grazie Bella, you always know how to cheer me up," he complimented, "How are things at the office?"

"Your wonderful workers here find me exasperating," I said with a slight hint of sarcasm.

"Don't pay attention to them; they are just jealous because you are so good at your job," he remarked.

"Mmm, I can understand Gina being apprehensive but the rest of them?" I whined.

"Don't worry about them, Bella. Things will settle down once they get used to your new position. Now, how did the meeting with the client go?" He inquired changing the subject.

"We got the contract," I declared lightening up.

"Eccellente! Brava ragazza, good girl, now this is what I am talking about; they are just jealous because you are brilliant at your job and they know it. That is why you got the promotion. It was for no other reason; don't you forget it. We have been trying to land that contract for years and Gina tried to no avail. You have been with us less than a year and within a month you got it, bravo. The difference between you and Gina is that you love what you do and you are passionate about your work; that is why you are very successful at it," he said exuberantly.

I filled him in on how the meeting went and the terms and conditions I agreed to with the client. We also talked about how best to approach the crisis he was faced with in New York. After discussing a few different ideas, we came up with an option we both felt would be best.

"I miss you, Bella," said Gianni.

"I wish you were here with me. It sure would've made this business trip a lot more pleasurable."

"Oh! Yeah.... like Gina and the rest of the girls here don't have enough to talk about and besides who will run the office?" I asked.

"Don't answer that; any way you will be back in a couple of days," I said reassuring him.

"Bellissimo, two more days away from you is too long, don't you miss me?" he whimpered.

"Of course I miss you, darling. The office is not the same without you and I can't wait for you to come back," I said flirtatiously.

"I have some more calls to make before I go to lunch, I have to go now, and you are keeping me away from my work."

"I won't tell the boss if you don't," he said wittily, both of us laughed.

"La mia stella! - You are a star! Alright, I will let you go, are you meeting Mandy for lunch?"

"Not sure yet. She is working on a new high profile case and meeting with the family now. She will call me when she is done," I replied.

"Okay, have a nice lunch and take care cara mia," he said putting down the phone. After my conversation with Gianni, I contemplated on how we met and what a small world we lived in.

Mandy and I attended a ball for charity the previous year when I was still modelling. I had decided to give up modelling and concentrate on a career; otherwise, my degree would have been a waste. The ball was held by one of the socialites and I was hired to model for the fashion show. My agent called and begged to do that one last job for her as it was a special request. Curious to know who was requesting for me, I accepted the job. There were so many different types of people there; from politicians to singers, high society, royalty and businessmen and women. It was quite an elegant event. Mandy and I were so excited; it was our first ball. I say our first but really it was Mandy's first time as I had been to a few though not as posh. The ball wasn't cheap; the ticket alone was so expensive I decided to buy it for Mandy to her relief. I didn't need a ticket but I still had to cover my expenses for a new outfit. I wanted to stay away from the usual sexy look and go for a princess look. Ever since Mandy and I were little, we always dreamt of dressing up like princesses going to a ball and meeting our Prince Charming. Now that this charity ball presented itself to us, we wanted to make sure we looked the part and make our dreams come true.

Mandy and I did nothing but talk about the ball, planning what we would wear and what hair style to have; we were on cloud nine. Naturally, we got on Tracey's nerves going on about the ball. It was not really her kind of event and she could not afford it even if she wanted to go. Joanne, on the other hand, was used to attending that kind of event and would have loved to attend if not that she had planned on traveling to Dubai for a week.

First thing Saturday morning, Mandy and I hit the shops to look for our ball gowns. We had fun trying on so many gowns of different colors. We saw few that were just simply gorgeous but their prices were out of Mandy's range; there was nothing there less than a thousand pounds and we had to buy shoes and handbags, too. Feeling dejected, we decided to go for a drink to cheer ourselves up. We felt much better after a few glasses of wine. We began talking about getting our nails done; though I could have offered to buy the gown for Mandy, I didn't want her to feel embarrassed as it would seem as if she could not pay her way to the ball. Already, I had bought her the ticket. I tried not to make her feel like I earned more than her unlike Joanne who rubbed her wealth on our faces making Tracey and Mandy feel inadequate. I suggested she hired the ball gown instead; which she was happy to consider an option. Sipping my glass of red wine, I took out my mobile phone to call Joanne to ask her if she wanted to go clubbing later; she agreed.

After making that arrangement, we had one more glass of wine and went to book an appointment for our hair and nails to ensure we got the date and time we wanted and to avoid last-minute hiccups. We went into the shoe shops and had a look at some shoes. We had to resist the temptation to buy any as we were not yet sure of the gown we would wear; we left for home instead.

The day of the charity ball drew closer and Mandy still did not have her ball gown. She was stressing out; the option to hire was even expensive. Luckily for me during the fittings, I saw a beautiful Ivory and gold dress with strapless neckline, fitted bodice and big skirt. The bodice was accented with lace applique and the detachable ribbon flower at the waist accents the stunning ball gown, with lace embellishment at the skirt and the hemline. I was in love. I asked Fame Star, the designer, if I could try it on and she agreed. She helped me put on the dress. Facing her, she gasped in delight covering her mouth. She showered me with compliments saying that I looked breath-taking and the dress was made just for me. I went to look at myself in the mirror and I felt like a princess.

I held my head up high and asked, Fame Star, "May I wear it to the ball?"

"You must!" she said; she was only too happy as it was one of her latest designs.

Mandy borrowed one of Joanne's gowns but I managed to convince her that since I was not buying my ball gown, anymore I might as well use the money to buy it for her instead. The dress I bought for her was a beautiful strapless A-line silhouette gown with a corset closure Empress Taffeta and sweetheart neckline. It was asymmetrically-draped and had fitted bodice accented with embellished lace motifs.

At last, the day of the ball arrived. The plan was to go ahead of Mandy to get ready for the show but she wanted to come with me. I took a cab to her house to pick her up. She came out looking stunning clad in her dress. Yellow wasn't her color but she looked beautiful. After the fashion show, I came out and joined Mandy at the table. The music was playing and a middle-aged man came over to ask Mandy for a dance; it was the Waltz. The quixotic music fell silent and I began to daydream and fantasize dancing with my prince.

In a distance, while lost in thought, I could hear a gentleman's voice asking, "May I have this dance?"

I thought I was still dreaming but the voice got louder. I looked up and there he was; my Prince Charming gazing down at me and reaching out for my hand. Without hesitation, I placed my right hand in his as I stood up. His eyes did not leave mine as he swept me across the dance floor; it was so magical I felt like I was in a fairy-tale.

After few more dances together, we finally introduced ourselves. He had the most romantic accent and highly captivating face. Everything about him was amorous. For a moment I thought I was in love. He left me briefly to attend to someone seeking his attention. As soon as he left, Mandy ran across to our table leaving the gentleman she was dancing with and blurted out, "Who is that?" checking him out.

"His name is Gianni," I responded with a big grin and with a feeling of butterflies in my stomach.

"The Gianni Canuti, owner of the biggest PR company in the city?" asked Mandy excitedly.

"I don't know; he just said Gianni," I replied. In no time, Gianni returned with a bottle of champagne.

We spent the rest of the evening in his company and we had so much fun. At the end of the ball, Gianni dropped us home; Mandy first then me. When we reached in front of my apartment, he walked me to the door but he did not want to come in. He kissed my hand and gazing into my eyes he said, "buonanotte amore mio – goodnight my love."

My heart skipped a beat and my knees could barely carry me. I heard myself whisper, "buonanotte," and then he left.

That night, I could not sleep as I thought about Gianni. He was the first man that had shown me so much respect and didn't want to come in for coffee except for Anthony though he didn't really count. When I finally slept, I dreamt of Gianni and me getting married, having babies and living happily ever after. While I was still in deep thoughts, Annabel knocked at my office door which brought me back to the present day. She wanted to know if it was alright for her to go to lunch. I nodded in agreement. As Annabel was leaving I asked, "Has Mandy called?"

"No," she replied as she exited through the door. I picked up the receiver to dial Mandy's number and she was on the line.

"That was quick," she said in reference to the speed of which I picked up the phone.

"I was just going to call you," I declared.

We agreed to meet up for lunch at our usual place, Carluccio's Restaurant which was not far from both our offices. I called and booked a table for two.

We met outside the restaurant, greeted each other with a kiss and a hug. As we entered, the head waiter, Stefano, greeted us in his usual manner, "Ciao, bella ragazza'come stai oggi? - Hello, beautiful, how are you today?" He asked cheerfully.

"Bene grazie," I replied.

"Fine thank you, Stefano," replied Mandy flirtatiously.

"Your table," he said walking us to our usual table.

"Grazie," I said sitting down. He pulled the chair out for Mandy to sit down and as she did, she thanked him and gave him an alluring smile. I wondered what was going on between them because he was equally reciprocating. As soon as he left our table, I lunged forward and said, "Spill!"

She began to laugh not revealing a thing; so I glared at her. "What?" she responded innocently.

I pulled back as if my feelings were hurt and started sulking.

"Alright, alright," she said grabbing my hands, "You know we went out a couple of times, right? Well, you know all the details about that. He called me last night and wanted us to start seeing each other again. He said that he loved and missed me and that I'm the most beautiful woman in the world…."

"Huh!" I expressed with a hint of cynicism interrupting her.

"Well, you know Italian men are always melodramatic," she said, dismissively. Anyway, there is nothing to tell; that's just it."

"What about Aden?" I asked slightly concerned. When her face lit up, I knew things were okay even before she said anything.

Mandy had been dating Aden for the past four months. I had never seen her so happy and in love like that before. It warmed my heart to see her deliriously in love. I really hoped things worked out for them.

"How are you coping without Gianni at the office?" She asked.

I rolled my eyes with an exasperated expression at the thought of the attitude of my work colleagues.

"The women in that office are so antagonistic; it's unreal. I mean I have no problem with the men there at all; they are so helpful. But that Gina, I am sure she thoroughly lives just to be a thorn in my side," I answered.

"Come on, Sandy! You know she is only jealous," she said empathetically.

"Gianni said the same thing," I responded, and then I thought for a split second then continued. "I ended my relationship with him to avoid all this; remember how I felt when I found out he was my new boss?" casting my mind back a year ago.

Not long after the ball, Gianni and I started dating. It was magical; he was everything I wanted in a man. Everything happened so fast: He came to my house the following morning after the ball with breakfast on a silver tray, freshly squeezed orange juice, croissants, scrambled eggs, bread rolls and a red rose between his teeth. I was still lying in bed when I heard a knock at my front door. I looked through the window to see who it was. I was shocked and delighted to see Gianni standing there. I rushed to the bathroom quickly to freshen up. I dabbed lip gloss on my lips, a quick brush of the hair then ran to the door with my cream nightdress and robe on. I took a deep breath then opened the door posing seductively.

"Good morning," I greeted as casually as I could, hoping he would not notice how apprehensive I was feeling inside yet very aroused. His eyes travelled up and down my body. I could barely control myself. He took the rose from his mouth and uttered, "Wow!" I was pleased with his reaction but tried to act unshaken.

"You look more beautiful now than last night," he complimented.

I smiled shyly, moving my hand to let him in. I led him to the sitting room.

"I got you breakfast, Amore mio, my love," gazing into my eyes. I reached out to take the tray from him and our fingers brushed gently; I felt electricity travel all over my body. Still holding his gaze, I longed for him to kiss me.

"Thank you," I said softly.

I turned around to put the tray on the table; I could feel him so close behind me. My mouth was dry and I'm sure my hands were sweaty, too. I felt like a teenager on a first date. I put the tray down on the table and was about to turn around when I felt his hand move my hair from the nape of my neck and he sensuously planted a kiss there. Unable to control myself, I spun around and we kissed passionately nearly knocking down the breakfast tray. We kissed for what seemed like hours and making love right there on the sofa. We spent the whole day making love. We went from the sitting room to a soapy bath in the tub; on to the bedroom and on the kitchen table; we couldn't get enough of each other. He didn't go home; we spent the whole weekend together. Although we didn't do much talking, we were comfortable and content with each other; it was as if we had known each other forever. He left first thing on Monday morning because he had to be at work by 8:30 am. I also was starting a new temp assignment at 10 am that morning. We arranged to meet up after work about 7 pm for dinner. As soon as he left my bed, I was missing him already and I didn't even know his surname or what he did for a living but I didn't care; he was just perfect.

Once I was ready for work, I looked at my diary to find out the name of the place my employment agency had got me working for the next four weeks as I decided to give up modelling and concentrate on my career. When I arrived at the office, I was highly impressed with the place; it was nice, big and very organized. I thought, "How great it would be to work here permanently." A pretty blond-haired lady approached me and introduced herself as Gina. She told me I would be working with her. She was friendly and showed me around; she introduced me to the other workers then took me to the boss's office. When we entered his office, the chair was backing us. She began to introduce me so he swang his chair around to greet me. His facial expression was shocked and speechless; I too was shocked but quickly composed myself and greeted him as if meeting for the first time. Gina picked up on something and asked if we had met before to which I quickly answered. "It must have been from one of the fashion shows I had modelled for or some catalog magazine when I was younger."

"So you are a model then?" Gina asked.

"Oh, I did some work here and there; nothing big," I said playing it down as not to be disrespected in the office. I couldn't make eye contact with Gianni but I could feel his eyes piercing through me. Once Gina finished the introduction and we were leaving, I said, "Nice to meet you, Mr. Canuti." Still unable to speak, he nodded his head and swang his chair round backing us again.

"He's not always like that; he's really nice," Gina said defensively. I smiled sheepishly. Half of the morning was spent with Gina training me. I tried so hard to concentrate and not think of what had just happened; Gianni being Mr. Canuti, my new boss. "The Gianni Canuti," of the biggest public relations companies in the city. My mind raced on what to do so I decided that after that day, I would not work there anymore even though it was a great place to work. I remembered applying for a job there right after university but I was turned down; nevertheless as soon as I was able, I would ring my agency to ask them to find a replacement for tomorrow. It was so hard to be near Gianni and not talk to him or touch him. Finally, it was lunch time. As soon as I left the office, I called Mandy as I was filling her in on everything. I heard Gianni's voice behind me, "Come stai amore mio? - How are you, my love?"

I turned around as I was happy to see him. We embraced and kissed passionately as if we hadn't seen each other for a very long time. I totally forgot that Mandy was still on the phone. In the distance, I could just about hear Mandy's voice saying, "Hello, hello, Sandy, Sandra?" I turned off my phone still kissing Gianni. He took me to Carluccio's Restaurant for lunch. All the staff there were very friendly. They seemed to know him very well as if they were family. Once we were seated at our table, there was an uncomfortable silence because we had so many questions to ask each other. I was waiting for him to start while he also wanted me to initiate a conversation. Finally, I broke the silence and said, "So you are the Mr. Canuti of the PR world?" He laughed and replied, "I wouldn't say that."

"Modest, too, I liked that," I said, playfully nodding my head which caused him to smile shyly. "My, my, Mr. Canuti are you blushing?" teasing him further.

He took my hands, lifted them to his lips, maintaining eye contact and kissed them. "I feel so nervous when I am around you," he said. "My heart won't stop racing. I feel like a little school boy again," taking my hand to his beating heart.

"I feel the same," I replied, stroking his face lovingly.

We discussed a lot of things during our meal. I told him my plan to stop working for him as it would be awkward, but he disagreed. He thought it would be a lot of fun working side by side so I told him I would work for a week and see how it went. I didn't want anyone there know that I was dating the boss. We were having such a great time that I almost forgot that my lunchtime was over. So I got up quickly to head back to the office but Gianni insisted that I finish my food and drink. I told him I couldn't as I must get back because it doesn't look good for my first day to be late. Even though he was the boss, I did not want any special treatment. Kissing him quickly and thanking him for my lunch, I ran back to the office. I just about made it back on time; thank God the restaurant was not far from the office. I put a couple of mints in my mouth to hide the champagne I drank. For the rest of the afternoon Gina showed me all the things I needed to know until she was confident that I could work on my own. She was very affable and supportive. I enjoyed working with her.

The week went fast. Surprisingly, I loved the job and I was very good at it. Everyone there was nice and helpful especially the men; which annoyed Gianni at times because he was jealous. It didn't help when one of them asked me out. I overheard Gina singing my praises to Gianni and suggested that they should offer me a permanent position; an opportunity he jumped at just to have me around. In less than a month, I signed a contract with them. Gina and I worked well together and we became friends in the process. She taught me a lot about the job and said I brought fun to the workplace. For me, that was easy because I loved what I did and I found I was very good at it which took Gianni by surprise. Gina suggested that we all went out after work to celebrate my becoming a permanent member of staff.

At the bar, Gina bought me a bottle of champagne. Gianni also bought me few more bottles. As the evening wore on, we got merrier and it got harder to mask the fact that Gianni and I were seeing each other. Gina noticed us looking at each other few times; gradually, her attitude changed. She started to ingratiate to Gianni which left me to feel unease. That emboldened her to link arms with him and leaned her head on his shoulder. Confused by what was going on, I knocked back my drink fearing the worst. Gianni was concerned and diplomatically removed her arm from his. Not pleased with that, she gave me a quick glance, then kissed him passionately on the lips. I couldn't tell whether he responded or not but that didn't matter. I felt like someone had just pierced my heart with a knife. I could not hide my hurt and jealous expression. I stood up abruptly and rushed to the toilet as I held back my tears. Not long after, Gina followed and I pretended to have eyelash inside my eye. She did not waste any time. With one hand on her hip she asked right out in an angry tone: "What is going on with you and Gianni?"

I was still facing the mirror blinking fast as if to move the eyelash from my eye. "I don't know what you are talking about," I answered. "Can you pass me a tissue, please? My eye," acting as if it was really bothering me and hoping to change the subject but she wasn't falling for it.

"Do you think I'm stupid? I saw the way you were looking at him all night; don't deny it," she persisted.

I sighed. Knowing she was not going to let it go, I turned to face her. Seeing how hurt she was, I couldn't bring myself to tell her the truth. I told her that she was right that I had a little crush on Gianni but that was all and I probably embarrassed him and made a fool of myself in front of everyone not to mention feeling stupid for having a crush on the boss. Hoping that she bought the story, I started crying and couldn't stop. She consoled me and told me not to worry as I was not the first person to fall for the boss, giving me a hug. She told me that she had been going out with Gianni for three years. My eyes widened at the shock of her revelation. My heart sank; I felt like I couldn't breathe. Gina realized something was wrong and released me from the hug holding my arms.

"Are you alright?" She asked looking concerned.

"I am so sorry I meant no harm. I did not know you guys were a couple," I said apologetically then I burst out crying again.

"I feel so bad, no one told me," I said feeling the weight of betrayal by Gianni.

"Everyone in the office knows. I thought you knew too," she said.

"It's okay, don't worry about it. He is someone you can easily fall for. He's good-looking, charming, rich and powerful. I don't blame you; other girls have fallen for him in the past but no one has gotten between us. Come on, clean up your face and let's go and get a drink. Men should never get between friends; sorry for the way I acted."

Having a drink was the last thing I needed but as I was retouching my makeup, I thought it could be a blessing in disguise. What if things didn't work out down the line then I would lose my job that I loved so much? With that in mind, I decided to get plastered and had a jolly good time. I removed the clip from my hair letting the big curls cascade down my shoulders and changed my color lipstick to scarlet red adding lip gloss.

Pouting my lips, I shook my hair, and took off my dress suit jacket. I felt free and sexy looking at myself in the mirror. Since I started working at the office, I had always worn a suit and pinned my hair up and always wore light makeup in order to fit in at the office and to be taken seriously. I decided from then to dress glamorous and sexy to work every day. I was going to show Gianni what he was missing and could not have. I took out my Channel No. 5 bottle of perfume Gianni bought me the past week and sprayed on my wrist and dabbed behind my ears. I then sprayed some on my hair. I turned around to face Gina who had been watching the transformation.

"Voila!" I said, opening my arms wide striking a pose.

"Wow! She exclaimed, you really do look like a model and I think I have seen you on television or magazine; you look great."

I linked my arm through hers.

"Come on let's go and have some fun," I said flashing the biggest smile I could.

As we emerged from the ladies', I got some admiring stirs from people especially the men. Even though I had not modelled for a while, I still got recognized by the public. Gianni and some of our work colleagues were still sitting down while others were dancing. When Gianni saw us approaching, for a moment, I thought I saw fear in his eyes. Ignoring him, my glance shifted to Justin who had asked me out a couple of weeks ago in the office.

His mouth was opened wide as if he had not seen me before. In fact, all of them were agape at my transformation. I gave Justin a flirtatious smile as I sat down; giving Gianni a quick glance. He had tightened his jaw muscles looking unimpressed by my action.

I continued flirting and dancing provocatively with a handsome chap ignoring him completely. Gianni tried to corner me and talk a number of times but I avoided him on all occasions. Late into the night, many of my colleagues had gone home. I had a lot to drink but I was not drunk. Gina, Annabel, Justin, and Gianni were still there. By 11:30 pm, Gianni offered to take me home to ensure that I got home safely as he did not want anything bad to happen to one of his new employees. I declined and insisted that I was going to stay until closing time. He insisted on waiting as well. Gina insisted she too was staying.

I put my foot down and told them both to go home that I could take care of myself. Just then the guy I was dancing with came back with more drinks for both of us. I gave him a snog to thank him for the drink then turned back to Gianni and Gina and told them that I had company and would be fine getting home. Gianni was reluctant to leave but Gina dragged him assuring him that I was going to be fine. As soon as they left, I knocked my drinks back and called a cab. On my way home, I called Mandy but she did not pick her phone so I called Anthony, with a sleepy voice, he said, "Hello, Sandra."

"How do you know it's me?" I asked trying to sound cheery

"Because no one else calls me this late," he replied in a deep husky voice.

"Are you drunk?"

"No!" I replied, slightly hurt by his question.

"So who is it this time that has broken your heart?" he asked.

I could no longer carry on with the facade so I burst out crying. The taxi driver looked at me through the mirror to check and see if I was okay while Anthony was trying to comfort me on the phone. I told him I would call him back as a call from Mandy was coming through. I answered Mandy's call and filled her in on everything that took place in the bar. She wanted to come to my house to make sure I was okay but I told her I was on my way to Anthony's and would spend the night there in case Gianni turned up at my doorstep. I wasn't ready to hear anything he had to say.

Saturday afternoon, I went back home to find that Gianni had bombarded me with calls on my landline; I refused to pick up his calls on my mobile phone. On top of it all, he had left a big bouquet of red roses and card at my doorstep. I knew it was him when I heard a knock on my door. I was not going to open the door but he was very persistent, then he started shouting through the letterbox that he was not going away and he knew that I was in there as he saw me go in. Fuming, I opened the door.

He pushed past me straight to the sitting room; he looked like he was about to explode. I closed the door and followed behind angry that he was angry.

"How could you do this to me?" he yelled waving his hand in the air looking so hurt.

Then I yelled back, "How could you do this to me?" and started crying. His face softened.

"Did you sleep with him?" He queried.

"Did you sleep with her?" Throwing the question back at him looking betrayed.

"Oh bella mia- my beautiful one," he said, wiping away my tears. "What did Gina tell you?"

"It's what you didn't tell me that was more important" I replied angrily moving away from him and flopping down on my sofa.

He sat down next to me breathing out deeply. He covered his face then ran his hands through his hair. Turning to me he cupped my face with his left hand and gazed into my eyes deeply. Captured and mesmerized by his piercing eyes, I felt myself weakening again. He looked so tired and unshaven as if he had not slept all night yet I could see love in his eyes. Could my heart be deceiving me or I was seeing what I wanted to see? Was I falling in love with him?

"You know how much I love you," he said sincerely, almost in tears.

"Ti amo, amore mio- I love you darling, please believe me. From the moment I met you, I fell madly in love with you."

Whatever it was about him that pulled me towards him terrified me. I longed to reach out and hold him but Gina's words were ringing in my ears.

"What about you and Gina?" I managed to ask.

"There is no me and Gina," he replied quite angered by my question.

"That's not what it looked like last night," I said standing up angrily, "I have never been hurt like the way you hurt me, seeing you kiss her."

"She kissed me!" He said defensively cutting me off in a thick Italian accent.

"I did nothing wrong but you.... you smashed my heart into tiny little pieces. I call and you don't pick; I knock on your door and there's no answer. Look at me; I slept inside my car out there waiting for you all night. When you didn't come, I was worried then I got angry and felt like dying. Now you came back this afternoon and my brain wanted to explode because I had all these images running through my mind."

He grabbed my arms firmly and pleaded.

"Per favore Tesoro - please darling, tell me, did you sleep with him; darling did you?"

"Slept with whom?" I asked knowing fully well whom he was referring to.

"Don't toy with me," he snapped giving me a shake in exasperation, then continued "The man you kissed in the bar and did not come home until now, did you sleep with him?" he asked. I could feel his grip on my arms tightening as he waited in anticipation for the answer.

"No!" I answered.

He hugged me tightly with a deep sigh of relief and then he started to plant kisses over my face. When he stopped, he asked me where I was all night. So I informed him that I spent the night at my friend's knowing he would try to come to my place. I told him I was too angry to hear what he had to say and as soon as he left with Gina, I called a cab and left on my own. He articulated that there was nothing between him and Gina. They used to be lovers but he ended it six months ago but she would not accept it. He said that the relationship died two years ago but she still tried to cling on.

"I kind of pity her really but if she wasn't so good at her job I would have gotten rid of her ages ago. She acts like she owns me and everybody should know it," he said thoughtfully as if realizing it for the first time.

He explained their relationship to assure me that there was nothing between them anymore. He could see I was not convinced.

"Okay!" he said taking out his mobile phone and made a call putting it on speaker. To my surprise, it was Gina. I shifted uncomfortably and was about to speak when he signaled for me to be silent as he spoke to her. After the conversation, it became very clear to me there was nothing between them.

I was surprised at how she could lie to me like that. I felt pity for her not being able to let go of Gianni. During their conversation, he cautioned her about her behavior and she apologized. When he put the phone down, I regretted the way I behaved and for not believing him. I couldn't say anything but kiss him lovingly. We ended up making love.

While Gianni showered and shaved, I made him something to eat. We talked about what had happened and where to go from there. He stated that all that would not have happened if we had been open about our relationship from the start as he wanted. I made it known to him that I needed time to think things over to decide what would be the best course of action to take. After lunch, he went home and wanted us to go out to dinner in the evening but I declined; I had already made an arrangement to attend church with Tracy in the morning and needed an early night. I assured him that I would call him Sunday evening by which time I would know what to do about the relationship and the office situation.

In the end, I decided to end things with Gianni and stay as friends. I didn't want to complicate things in the office or cause animosity between Gina and me. She was very popular in the office and I liked her and didn't want to hurt her. I wanted to concentrate on my career, maybe Gianni and I were not meant to be. I dreaded telling him so I told him on the phone because I knew I could not go through with it face to face. He did not take the news well.

He did all he could to talk me out of it threatening to sack Gina. He insisted on coming around to sort it out face to face but I refused. I was adamant that it was over. He said he would never give up on me.

"Sei l'amore della mia vita - you're the love of my life, I will wait until you are ready. I know in my heart we are meant to be together perhaps we met too early though I don't believe it. Whatever it is, I know you love me and I love you, so I will let you fly and when you are ready, you will come back to me" he said putting down the phone.

I knew he was crying. I knew I had hurt him terribly but I felt I made the right decision no matter how much it hurt. I cried myself to sleep. I didn't have the energy to even call Mandy. I did not want to talk to anyone and I did not want to be comforted. The next Monday morning was one of the worst days of my life. Gianni did not come to work the entire week. Gina was in charge and was as happy as she could be. It's as if she had won the lottery; that added to my sorrow. If only she knew the sacrifice I had made for her! I was relieved when the week was over. I just wanted to go home and shut myself away for the whole weekend but the girls would not let me. Joanne, Mandy, and Tracey coerced me to meet up for a drink after work to cheer me up.

Shaking off the memory from the past, I faced Mandy with great determination and said: "You know what, I am not going to take it from Gina anymore." I took a sip of my wine and continued, "She is going to see a different side of me henceforth. She may have been the reigning queen in our office but her time of reign is over. A new queen now sits on the throne and I am going to let her know that she has been dethroned. I am going to make her regret ever crossing me."

We had a lovely lunch but we had to cut it short to head back to our respective offices. We said our goodbyes and headed back to work.

Sunk into Work

People think gaining a promotion automatically makes things great and wonderful; but not in my case. To me, it meant working three times harder than before; prove to myself and others that I deserved the promotion. In my case, I needed to work even harder than before to put Gina in her place and to show Gianni and the rest of my colleagues that I was not just a pretty face. Of course, I knew Gianni didn't see me like that. Nevertheless, in order for me to retain my crown as the reigning queen, I had to work harder than the rest. I threw myself into my work for the next few months. I worked tirelessly going in early and leaving late. I didn't even have time for my friends and they were not too happy about it. Gianni was also concerned though secretly I knew he was proud of me. He would stay back with me working late on some nights. One Friday night, past

7 pm while I was still working, he came into my office. I didn't even notice him standing there watching me.

"You know you have nothing to prove, Cara mia," he said.

Startled, I looked up smiling at him as he walked towards my desk. I rolled my shoulders backward feeling fatigue. He went behind me and started massaging my shoulders. It felt so good I didn't want him to stop.

"You work too hard," he said.

"I have never met anyone who worked as hard as you do. Come on! It is time to call it a day," sitting on top of my desk.

"Well, you should be very happy to have someone so dedicated. I mean, what is the world coming to when the boss tells the employee not to work so hard?" I said humorously.

"You know I hate it when you refer to me as your boss," he said frowning at me and looking deeply into my eyes. He continued, "You mean more to me than this entire company."

Clearing my throat and breaking away from his gaze as my heart began to pound, I started to rustle with some papers on my desk. Suddenly he got up.

"Come on, I am taking you out to dinner."

And before I could object, he added, "I will not take no for an answer because I know you did not have a lunch break today."

He walked around to where I was sitting and pulled me up to my feet.

"Alright, alright," I said, freeing my hands in surrender.

"I am very hungry come to think of it. I guess I got so caught up with work that I didn't feel it." I gave him a peck on the cheek thanking him for caring and grabbed my handbag and jacket.

"Where are we going?" I asked. "I hope it is not somewhere too fancy. I'm not dressed for the part."

"You can be dressed in a rag and still look bellissimo; come on let's go. It's a Friday night. Let's go out and have some fun. You've been working too, too hard the past few months," he complimented.

"No, no, no; I can't stay out too late. I have some paperwork to do. I need them for a meeting on Monday," I protested. He interrupted me and said in a protracted manner, "Sandra, life is for the living. Where has that fun-loving girl gone to? You are neglecting your friends; you don't have time for me anymore; it's like all you care about is work, work, work and more work; what is really going on?"

I could see where this conversation was leading so I told him I would go out and have fun with him. I went to the bathroom and freshened up then we left for dinner. I was pretty quiet through dinner as I couldn't really switch off and relax.

"Don't you like the food?" he asked looking worried.

"Mmm…the food's lovely," I replied putting a bite in my mouth.

"Then it's the company," he said looking dejected.

"No, the company is perfect," I reassured him stroking his face lovingly.

He cupped my hand on his face taking it to his lips and kissed it.

"il mio amore - my love, please tell me; what can I do to make you happy?" He asked, still holding on to my hand across the table.

"I am happy; I'm happy with what I am doing, I love my job," I replied.

"Maybe too much; there's a lot more to life than work. You need to relax a bit. Take a holiday. Since you started working for the firm you have never had a day off. I insist you take some time off," he said austerely. I took back my hand slightly offended

"Are you ordering me as my boss or…?" I began to ask.

"No, of course not!" he replied cutting in and slightly angered by my question.

"I care about you and you know that. I know you need a break even if you don't know it."

I rolled my eyes in exasperation tired of him going on about it. Seeing my expression, he changed the subject and we discussed lighter matters throughout dinner. By the end of dinner, I was a lot more relaxed and felt like my old self again but that was mainly due to the Champagne and wine we had with our meal. We went on to a club where we had such an amazing night. Gianni really did know what I needed.

Christmas holidays came and went which was our busiest time of the year. It was beginning to look like I was living in my office. We had so much work that some of the workers started to complain about the workload and having to stay and work overtime. I even heard some of them calling me a slave driver. I made the work place hell for Gina; I made her look ordinary before the other workers in the office. I exposed her antics and her flaws for all to see. The other girls who once sided with her against me now disregarded her and showed ample respect towards me. I knew the only way to get her was to prove myself and work harder. If I had given in to Gianni's wish to be open about our relationship while working there, I would have gained no respect from any of them.

Our firm won consultancy of the year award which meant more work. It felt like I had not seen the girls in years and Gianni seemed to spend less and less time at the office; not that I could blame him as a guy could only take so much knock backs, I guess. Since he promoted me to the position of manager, he spent more time in the New York office. I even heard a rumor about him seeing someone else.

Looking down at the PR weekly magazine with me on the front cover with the headline, "Formidable Sandra Appleton PR Queen" and the award on my desk we won for excellence, nothing but joy filled my heart. Our firm won UK consultancy of the year again. Winning the award put me and my work in the spotlight – highlighting my success to my peers, our clients, and our competitors. Industry awards gave us a competitive edge – helping us to win new business and retain our client accounts. The office was doing incredibly well. Tears began to form in my eyes; had I sacrificed love for my career? What about my friends and Anthony? Had I paid a high price to be where I am today? I had achieved in three years what it normally took people ten years to achieve in their career. I should be on top of the world yet here I was filled with regret. I thought I knew what was best for me. Was my aim too high? Did I want to have it all and ended up losing the most important things? The following month would have been our three years' anniversary and the firm's annual ball which I started two years ago to show our workers and clients our appreciation and to generate new clients. I began to cry; just then Gina knocked and came into my office with some papers for me to sign.

"Are you alright?" She asked, not that she cared.

Clearing my throat and composing myself I replied, "I'm fine," as she approached.

"What is it?" I was rather straight with her but I didn't care.

"I brought the papers you wanted," she answered.

"Leave them there," I said pointing at my desk.

"Sorry, I don't mean to pry but is everything alright?" She stopped to ask again on her way out.

"I know I'm probably the last person you want to confide in but we used to be friends once and I'm a really good listener." Softening my face and letting my guard down I said, "It is lonely at the top."

She sat down, "Please don't take offense but is it about Gianni?" she asked. I was disconcerted by her question.

"I know you love him and he claims to be in love with you," she went on. All these years, you both tried to hide it but everyone here knows it. Don't get me wrong but I think it is honorable that you didn't take it further though if he truly loved you he would have taken you to his family home like he did with me to meet his parents."

When she did not get a reaction from me she continued.

"I take it that he has never introduced you to his parents, right?" I was unable to answer her but by my expressions, she knew I hadn't met them and that seemed to please her slightly; then I knew she was my nemesis.

"I have some work to get on with," I said coldly dismissing her but before she left she added, "I wouldn't feel bad if I were you; just like he led me and you on the garden path, I'm quite sure he will do the same to his new blonde bombshell in New York," she gave a circuitous smile then left.

Incensed by her comment, I decided to send her to our office branch in Shanghai, meaning she was going to miss out on the ball the coming month. That would serve her right. She had to know by then not to mess with me. As soon as Gina left my office, I asked Annabel to book me the first available flight to New York and reschedule all my appointments. She got me a morning flight. I called Mandy to ask her if she could meet me at mine. She was surprised to hear from me as I had not spoken to her in a couple of weeks or more which was very unusual. She came with takeaway because I did not have anything to eat. We spoke briefly about things; I assured her that things were going to change upon my return the following week. After helping me pack, she left. I went to bed immediately as my flight was early in the morning.

I wore my classy but sexy short Nina Ricci dress that Gianni bought me the previous Christmas. I got to New York before 3 pm. I took a taxi straight from the airport heading to the office. I made sure that Gianni would be in the office on my arrival. Notwithstanding, I had been to that branch few times so I was not overly familiar with the workers but they seemed to know me very well and welcomed me with delight. As I was going to leave my luggage with the secretary, I saw the blond bombshell that Gina referred to. She smiled sweetly at me and I gave her a cold smile and headed towards Gianni's office which was upstairs with a clear glass window. I could see him up there on the phone and my heart leaped with anxiety and excitement. I had not seen him in two months and three days. I went up to his office and opened the door, posing seductively with a flirtatious smile.

"Ciao caro," I said.

He looked up. Shocked to see me, he told the caller that he would call back and put the phone down. He stood up and looked confused. I walked closer to him and put my arms around him. I kissed him passionately knowing full well that the office staff were watching. Feeling secure that he still wanted me, I stopped kissing him.

"I am sorry for all that I put you through and for turning up like a possessive girlfriend."

"I'm not," he said, kissing me with such hunger we forgot that we were not alone. Thank goodness for the secretary who called his phone to interrupt us. Giggling like a couple of schoolkids, we looked out to see the workers gawking at us; then Gianni closed the blinds. We kissed some more before heading off to the hotel he resided in. It was one of the well-respected hotels in the world, New York City's Hotel Plaza Rosa with its European grandeur and perfect location. Just one short block from Central Park and Madison Avenue on the Upper East Side; it was a shopper's dream.

Gianni had a presidential suite with the sumptuous décor of a European townhouse which was extremely spacious. The suite featured a master bedroom, separate living room with hardwood floors, large walk-in closet, and fully equipped kitchenette with microwave, stove, refrigerator, and coffeemaker. It had a master bathroom with dual sinks, separate shower, and deep soaking tub, additional half bathroom, dining room for eight people, plasma TV, and iPod docking station. This elegant hotel suite had the front facing views of the residences on this tree-lined Manhattan Street, not to mention a glass-enclosed atrium terrace and outdoor balcony with breath-taking views of the New York skyline.

It had everything a girl could dream of; every time I went there with Gianni, they treated us like royalty. The way the workers acted around him was as though he owned the hotel. "He must be a very good customer," I thought to myself. He whispered something to the hotel receptionist who gave him the card to his room door. The concierge followed us to the lift with my travel bags to the top floor of our suite. Gianni gave him a generous tip. Thanking him with gratitude, he left. I ran straight to the balcony looking out at the breath-taking view. "Oh! I love this place; it's so beautiful," I said.

"It holds no candle to your beauty, Cara," he said casually as he strolled towards me.

I turned around to face him; my heart filled with so much love for him. I nearly told him that I loved him but the words refused to come out so I just kissed him gently. While I unpacked my bags, he went and ran a bath for me as I expressed that I wanted to have a soak in the bathtub. After my bath, I came out dressed in the hotel white robe feeling refreshed and relaxed. I saw a beautiful romantic meal for two laid out on the table with a bottle of champagne. I raised my hands to my heart smiling tenderly at how thoughtful and romantic he could be. I went back to get dressed into something fitting for the occasion. I came out to find him sitting at the table. He rose up to pull back my chair like the gentleman he was.

While I went to sit down, he whispered in my ear sensually, "You look beautiful," planting a gentle kiss on my neck sending shivers through my body as I pinned my hair up like Audrey Hepburn in *Breakfast at Tiffany's*. I sat down and he handed me a glass of champagne whilst he sat down too. His eyes never left mine. He picked up his glass and raised it up:

"To us," he toasted as his eyes were filled with love.

"To us," I responded riveted as we gently clicked our crystal champagne glass together.

We both took a sip holding our gaze. All I wanted was to reach out and grab him and feel his body pressing against mine. As if reading my mind, he leaped forward and kissed me fervently. I reciprocated and we ended up in bedroom where we made love several times; we could not get enough of each other. I guess we were making up for all the wasted years. I forgot that I had not eaten since my plane landed. I felt famished and he was likewise drained after that entire workout. He ordered for new food to be brought up and more champagne though it was very late.

While we waited for the food, we took a shower together. The much-awaited food finally arrived. After eating, we went straight to bed. As I laid there in his arms, I felt so safe and loved. I could not imagine my life with anyone else; snuggling closer to him and holding him tight, he kissed my head and held me with both arms. Soaking in everything that had just happened in comfortable silence, Gianni called out my name softly.

"Sandra?"

"Mmm," I answered.

"Are you sleeping?" he asked.

"No," I replied.

He shifted to face me. He started to caress my face looking serious, "Ti amo con tutta l'anima - I love you with all my heart," he said.

Tears ran down my face as I was filled with emotion. I finally said the long and awaited word that I had never said to any man.

"I love you - Ti amo Gianni."

Overcome with delight, he hugged me so tight I could barely breathe but I did not care because I was filled with joy. I was sure I saw tears in his eyes. We slept in each other's arms until morning and it was the sweetest sleep I had ever had.

We spent the whole week getting to know each other again in every way. He took me everywhere shopping; 5th Avenue must have seen me coming. Gianni almost bought the whole shop. I had to restrain him from buying any more stuff for me. We went to our favorite Italian restaurant, Carluccio, just like the one near our office back in London; but this one was more posh and grand.

I wondered if it was the same owner. I didn't want to embarrass Gianni so I did not ask. They gave us a cordial greeting as always; even more so to Gianni as if they were family. Wherever I went with him, we were treated like royalty. I always felt like a princess whenever I was with him. Even more so now that our relationship was no longer a secret. I wanted the whole world to know that I was Gianni Canuti's girl. The week went so fast but we were both looking forward to going back to England and finally letting everyone know that we were officially together.

It was the last evening of our stay in New York. Gianni booked us a table downstairs in the hotel's restaurant. Just as I was picking the outfit to wear from amongst what he had bought me earlier in the week, he presented me with a big box wrapped in red ribbon.

"More gifts?" I asked with delight inquisitively.

"You spoil me too much," taking the box, I kissed him to thank him.

"I want you to wear this tonight. I want tonight to be perfect just like you are," he said stroking my face tenderly.

I opened the box excitedly and there was the most exquisite black dress by Jovani, one of my favorite designers. I lifted up the dress from the box in awe and gently slipped it on; the silk chiffon felt so good against my skin. This beautiful, feminine, classy, elegant strapless sweetheart evening dress with wrap skirt fell to the floor. Not to mention the embellishments: rhinestones, jewels, and beads.

As I admired myself in the mirror, Gianni came behind me and put on my neck the most beautiful diamond necklace I had ever seen. My heart began to pound because I knew this was Garrard's Heart of the Kingdom Ruby. The most expensive necklace in the world. It featured a 40.63-carat, heart-shaped Burmese ruby surrounded by 155 carats of diamonds. Burmese ruby was one of the most sought after varieties of ruby due to its blood-red hue. This gem was particularly valuable due to its extraordinary size. Burmese rubies rarely exceed a few carats.

This was priced $14 million. He turned to face me and inserted the pair of pear-shaped diamond earrings which weighed 60.1 carats altogether by Harry Winston, the most expensive earrings in the world, worth $8.5 million.

We handled some of the public relations for some of these companies and Gianni and I were looking at the catalogue collection playfully a while back as I imagined wearing them pretending to be a princess for a night like Cinderella. I wondered if he asked them whether he could borrow them for the night to fulfil my dreams. Carried away with the fairy-tale, I didn't want to spoil it by asking. He stepped back to inspect his handiwork then he led me to sit down on the bed. He left the room briefly then came back with a shoe box with glass slippers. They were studded with 565 Kwiat diamonds — 55 carats of clear diamonds and a single 5-carat gem and handbag to match. He knelt down in front of me and took my feet, he slipped the shoes on then he stood up.

"Mozzafiato! - Breath-taking!" he exclaimed.

"You are more than a princess," he continued pleased with his handiwork.

I stood up and looked in the mirror; it was like looking at someone else. I felt priceless; not because of all that I was wearing but because of how Gianni made me feel. I was close to tears thinking of how much effort he put in to make me feel like royalty. He held my shoulders giving them a gentle loving squeeze then he put his neck on my left shoulder as we were still looking in the mirror for a moment.

"Bella mia - my beautiful one, you take my breath away," he said kissing my neck tenderly as he left to finish dressing.

I stood speechless reflecting on a lot of things. At that moment he called out.

"We are leaving in five, Cara!"

I added the finishing touch to my dressing. I came out from the bedroom walking like the princess he had made me. Across from me was the most handsome prince I had ever seen. Dressed in a black tuxedo with a white shirt. I didn't think it was possible to love him any more than I did but looking at him standing there, I fell in love with him all over again. I didn't realize I was staring until he started to blush.

"You like?" he asked posing for me.

"I like very much," I replied.

There was a knock at the door.

"That would be our bodyguards," he said.

"Bodyguards?" I asked.

"A prince and a princess cannot go out without their bodyguards," he said jokingly as he went to open the door.

"Of course not," I replied in a royal manner smiling cheerfully.

"Are you ready, sir?" asked one of them.

"Yes," replied Gianni turning to look at me.

He reached out to take my hand and escorted me to the restaurant. The restaurant had a warm, soothing atmosphere accented with chiffon-colored walls, a gold-domed ceiling and murals of pagodas; everything was just sparkling beautiful. From the moment we walked out of the lift to the restaurant, all eyes were on us. The way all the workers of the hotel greeted was as if truly we were royalty. Some people gawped at us while some took pictures. The head waiter sat us down at our table which was more exclusive than the rest. Not long after we sat down, a man and a woman came over and asked for my autograph. I raised a speculative eyebrow at Gianni who eyed me to sign.

"I know I used to model three years ago but not to an international level like Kate Moss. I think they may have mistaken me to be some famous movie star," I said.

"Cara, you are more than a movie star. They are captivated by your beauty just like I am," he said kissing my hand tenderly.

A reporter snapped some shots of us but was quickly removed by our bodyguards.

"Wow!" I expressed in amazement. They really took their job seriously. Gianni gave a discreet nod at the headwaiter who moved swiftly towards our table.

"Your table is ready, sir. Please follow me," he said to Gianni. I looked at Gianni confused.

"You don't expect royalty to eat with her subjects, do you?" he said dashingly, "How unbecoming."

He smiled as he stood up and like a gentleman, pulled my chair out, I stood up gracefully. He put out his right arm for me so I linked mine with his and the headwaiter led us to a private room through the back of the restaurant. When the waiter opened the double doors, I gasped in awe. Rolled out was a red carpet that led to a single table in the center. There were pillar candles wrapped in raffia, twine, and satin ribbon all around the room with red stem roses. There sat at the corner of the room a pianist playing softly the most romantic classical piece of music I had ever heard. Arm in arm, we sauntered over to the very formal dinner table. The waiter pulled out the chair for both of us to sit down. Gianni did not once take his eyes off me. He watched every facial expression I made. I was lost for words; could the night get any better than that? I wondered; I wanted to pinch myself just to make sure that this was not a dream but I dared not as I didn't want to wake up.

Gianni squeezed my hand affectionately as if he read my mind. The waiter took the champagne, none other than Pernod-Ricard Perrier-Jouet. It was chilled in the silver bucket; he popped it open and poured for Gianni to taste. Once approved, he poured for both of us and left. I looked around the room at this private dinner setting; the two bodyguards stood at the door. The pianist was at the corner still playing; it was like a fairy-tale. I turned to face Gianni and was about to express my appreciation when he leaned across and kissed me gently on the lips and sat back down; his eyes were filled with love. He picked up his glass of champagne as I did.

"To the most beautiful woman in the world," he said.

"To the most handsome man in the world," I responded holding his gaze. The two champagne glasses clinched together and we took a sip of our champagne.

"I hope you don't mind that I ordered for you," he asked.

"Mr. Canuti, you can take me to the highest mountain and back and I wouldn't mind," I replied. He smiled.

We continued to admire each other until the waiters came with our food; a big silver-covered dish was placed in front of me and Gianni then they moved back and stood afar looking on. Gianni opened his and it looked delicious. I followed suit but was astounded by what was on my plate. I gave a quick glance at Gianni then back to my plate to make sure my eyes were seeing clearly or if I was imagining seeing a black ring box.

"Open it," he said calmly.

My heart started to beat really fast and my hands started to shake. I was almost too afraid to pick up the box. I looked up again at Gianni who sat there stiffly holding his breath. I picked up the box and opened it gently as he watched tensely. I gulped in amazement. Inside was 'The Chopard Blue Diamond Ring' set with an enormous, oval-shaped blue diamond. This expensive ring also had diamond shoulders and an 18k white gold band paved with diamonds. I was speechless.

Gianni came to me and knelt down on one knee taking my left hand.

"Sandra, sei la mia anima gemella - you're my soul mate," he said continuing, "siete la donna che più bella ho visto mai - you are my air, you are the most beautiful woman I've ever seen. From the moment I saw you, there was such a powerful connection between us I couldn't pull away even if I wanted. You saw I loved you then and I love you more now. Voglio passare il resto della mia vita con te, lo sposereste? - I want to spend the rest of my life with you, would you marry me?"

Moved by his words, tears ran down my face. I was speechless. I moved towards him and cupped his face with my hands and kissed him.

"Is that a yes?" He asked smiling.

"Yes!" I replied nodding my head with a beaming smile.

He slipped the ring on my finger and with great elation, he got up, carried me up and swang around overcome with joy.

"She said yes!" he proclaimed aloud.

The people in the room started clapping. He put me down and kissed me tenderly.

"Ti amo - I love you," I said.

"Ti amo troppo - I love you too," he replied still holding me in his arms.

We danced slowly to the beautiful music playing in the background. We were in a world of our own and had forgotten that people were in the room waiting on us. We did not realize that we had been there dancing for a long time until the head waiter cleared his throat to get our attention. Instead of going to eat, we headed back to our room holding hands as the bodyguards followed. The hotel restaurant was empty; the foyer was not as busy as it was earlier.

At last we were alone; I went to get changed and be Sandra Appleton again just to see if all that had happened was real. I gazed at the big engagement ring on my finger then held it to my heart. Gianni helped me remove the necklace while I took off the earrings and handed them over to him including the glass slippers. He left the room so I presumed he went to hand the jewelry back which was a relief because it was quite a responsibility wearing something that costly. Even still, it was great to be a princess for a night dancing with my Prince Charming.

I changed into something more comfortable letting my hair down. When I came out, there was a bottle of champagne and some food laid out on the table. We ate and drank celebrating our engagement. It must have been about 2 am or 3 am before we fell asleep after making love.

Chapter Eight

If Only I knew

Gianni was acting very strange; when we woke up in the morning I put on the TV, they were reading the news and he changed the channel quickly. When I asked why he simply replied that I was a lot more interesting to watch than any old boring news; he then kissed me. When we were leaving the hotel to head to the airport back to London, I saw a newspaper by the reception and wanted to have a glance but he abruptly ushered me away. He stated that we were running late and he did not want us to miss our plane. Whilst we were on the plane, the flight attendant was passing around today's newspapers and I wanted a copy but Gianni suddenly kissed me distracting me as the stewardess passed. This was the third time he had averted me seeing the news. I figured it might have been the reporter that took the photos of us last night; maybe he wrote something bad about me and he was trying to protect me from it so I did not press it.

A car picked us from the airport straight to my place. Gianni wanted us to go to his flat in Kensington which was a stunning and luxurious two-bedroom penthouse apartment with a lift. It has beautiful styling with state-of-the-art fittings and fixtures throughout; two en suite bedrooms, fantastic roof terrace, and a wonderful garden. The apartment was arranged over two floors and comprised an outstanding and light reception room with floor-to-ceiling windows and access to an amazing terrace, fabulous second reception room with stylish open-plan kitchen with fitted appliances, utility room, grand master bedroom with an incredible en suite bathroom with integrated TV which was my favorite part of the flat; not to mention the superb second bedroom with sleek bathroom, two guest cloakrooms and underground parking.

'It must have cost him an arm and a leg to rent that place,' I thought to myself but as nice as his place was, I didn't want to move in with him until after our wedding.

When we reached my place, I couldn't wait to call Mandy and the rest of the girls to share my wonderful news, plus I wanted to make up for not calling and spending as much time as we used to; I had really missed them. The last time we were all together like that was before Tracy's wedding to her long-time fiancé, John. It felt like old times again before I threw myself into my work. Immediately after the wedding, I went back to work and not having time for them again, but all that was going to change, especially my friendship with Mandy.

She had been my best friend since school and I had not been there for her the past two years even when I heard the rumors of the downturn of her relationship with Aden in the papers. I had been so wrapped up with trying to prove myself in the public relations world that I neglected her even though she had always been there for me. After we showered and had something to eat, Gianni went back to his. We arranged to go to his parents' for dinner later in the evening. I was quite nervous because it would be the first time I was meeting them. He reassured me that they were going to love me that I had nothing to worry about. I was still wracked with nerves. Unable to wait any longer to share my wonderful news to Mandy, I picked up the phone and dialed her number at home but she did not pick up.

I called her mobile and there was no answer either so I called Aden thinking she might be with him but he did not pick. I thought they might be otherwise engaged with some bedroom activities. I called Tracy and John who did not pick either, I began to get worried. I called Joanne who never let her mobile phone out of her sight; the phone scarcely rang before she picked.

"I will call you back," she said dropping abruptly.

Are they all in church? I wondered waiting anxiously but then what would Joanne be doing in church. I looked at the time, church service should have finished ages ago even if there was a special service. Then I thought to call Anthony though I did not really want to talk to him yet as I didn't know how to break the news to him about my engagement to Gianni. Nevertheless, I called him and there was no answer then I concluded that something was going on. The phone rang interrupting my thoughts; it was Joanne. Before I could say anything, she blurted out, "Don't you ever check your messages? We have left like gazillion messages on your phones."

"I just got in a couple of hours ago and I haven't turned on my mobile phone yet; what's up and where is everyone?" I asked apprehensively.

"Mandy is in the hospital," she replied with anxiety. I sat down fearing the worst.

"She was sent this morning by ambulance and she is still unconscious. We are all here in the hospital."

Every ounce of joy I felt moments ago was sapped out of me.

"What hospital?" I asked panicking as tears filled my eyes, not my Mandy, no. Once I got the name of the hospital I quickly got dressed not bothering to wear makeup. I grabbed my car keys and drove as fast as I could to the hospital. Upon my arrival, I saw the whole gang there waiting anxiously for the news. Aden was standing on his own, Tracey and John were standing together praying, Anthony and Joanne were sitting together comforting each other, and Mandy's parents were standing looking very fretful at the direction of the theater waiting for the doctor to come out with some news. As I walked swiftly towards them, Joanne jumped away from Anthony's arms and ran towards me and we embraced.

"Any news from the doctor?" I asked hoping for a positive report.

She shook her head sadly. I hugged and greeted the rest of them then I stayed with Mandy's parents holding her mom tightly. We all rushed towards the doctor as she came out.

132

"How is she, doctor? I asked jumping in first in distress.

"She is still unconscious and in a critical but stable condition. We are doing all we can. We managed to pump out the drugs and alcohol in her system. Her body is badly bruised but there are no broken bones. She is a tough girl," replied the doctor.

"Drugs? No broken bones? What in the world happened to her.....?" I asked bewildered.

"Can we see her now?" asked Mandy's mom cutting in.

"Yes but only the immediate family for now," replied the doctor.

Aden was about to go in when Mandy's mom glared at him stopping him in his tracks, then she pulled me to go in with them. Curious about what was going on with Aden and them, I wanted to stay and find out first so I told them to go on ahead I would be there shortly. Mandy's dad held his wife gently as they followed the doctor to the room.

No sooner had they left than I swang around, "Alright. What is going on here and what happened to Mandy?" I asked petulantly.

Everyone looked at Aden and he turned away guiltily. Frustrated and in need of an immediate answer, I turned to Tracey. She was flustered for a moment then she began to tell me but Joanne jumped in and declared that Aden tried to kill Mandy.

"What?" shocked by her revelation.

"He beat her to a bloody pulp in one of his drunken rages," said Joanne in a vehement manner.

"You mean to tell me Aden laid a hand on Mandy?" I asked

133

unable to believe what I had just heard. "And this has happened before?" They all shared a look between them with nobody answering.

"And no one told me?" Angry and hurt for not noticing what Mandy was going through and for not being there for her, I backed up and ran towards the private room Mandy was in. As I entered, her mom was leaning over her crying while the dad comforted her. At first, I could not see Mandy because her parents blocked my view. As I moved closer, I stopped dead in my tracks with my hands to my mouth. Tears ran down my face. There was Mandy, lying all hooked up to the machines. Her face black and blue swollen. I don't think I had ever been as scared in my life as I was seeing her like that. I stood there frozen. Her dad noticed me and came over putting his arms around me and took me over to the bed beside his wife. I couldn't take my eyes off Mandy. It was as though I was staring at someone else.

I sat down on the chair beside the bed and took Mandy's frail hand and rubbed my cheek still crying.

"Mand, it's me. I'm back! I'm so sorry I have not been there for you," I said.

"Remember before I went away I told you things would change when I come back? I promise from now on I am going to be there for you. I will never let you down again. Mandy and Sandra against the world, remember? Do you want to hear a joke? I'm going to quit my job, and do you want to know something else? Can you believe I left my house without makeup just now? There's one for the books? Well, you have to open your eyes to see this one to believe it but then you should know I would do anything for you. I'm rumbling on; you know I do that when I get scared and you usually tell me to…"

"Shut up!" said Mandy in a weak and faint voice cutting in.

"Mand, oh! Mand," I cried out with relief jumping up from the chair giving her a hug.

"Ouch," rang her enervated voice.

"Sorry," I said releasing her.

"Oh! My darling girl, you had us so worried," said her mom holding her and giving her a kiss.

"Hello baby. It's daddy. How is my little girl feeling?" asked her dad tenderly.

The doctor entered the room. After checking Mandy, she asked us to leave so Mandy could get some rest. We said our goodbyes promising to come back later. As soon as I left the room, I marched straight towards Aden with rage. Tracey and John plus Anthony and Joanne approached us anxiously wanting to know how Mandy was. Ignoring them, I threw a right hook on Aden's face which caused him to lose balance; he staggered back.

"Is this how you hit her?" I yelled, "Care to show? Or is this not private enough for you?" I said looking around. Everyone was watching but I didn't care.

"You are a coward, a sorry excuse of a man. She is worth more than ruby and you trampled all over her." I wanted to punch him again but Mandy's dad came and pulled me away from him.

"Come on love, he is not worth it," he said. Before I went with him, I issued a last warning to Aden.

"I warned you once that if you ever hurt Mandy I would

135

make you pay," I went right close to his face and said in a very cold manner.

"I always keep my word," then I walked away back to the others.

"She looks so hot when she's feisty," said Anthony to Joanne.

"I'm feisty," she replied a little jealous.

Since Mandy was stable, Tracey and John decided to head on home. Joanne also wanted to go with Antony but he was staying if I was; that did not please Joanne so she decided to stay too. For a moment, I wondered if something was going on between them but Mandy would have told me if there was. Mandy's mom came to take me aside.

"Look, love... you just came back from New York; you must be tired," she said sympathetically.

"No, I'm fine. I want to stay," I protested.

"I'm sure you do dear but there must be some other things you ought to be getting on with," she said looking at my engagement ring. I instinctively covered it with my right hand. I felt it was inappropriate to the current situation but she just smiled and gave me a hug and a kiss congratulating me.

"Now go on, I'm sure Gianni is waiting."

"Oh no Gianni. I totally forgot all about him," I said in frenzy.

"Can you say goodbye to the others for me? Please don't tell them about the engagement. I want to do it myself."

"Of course dear," she said with warmth and understanding.

Mandy's mom was like a second mom to me. Ever since Mandy and I became friends, she just liked me from the word go and has been there for me over the years. I gave her a kiss

136

and scurried. On my way, I called Gianni filling him in on everything. He wanted to postpone but I insisted we should go ahead as I longed to meet his parents at last. I texted Anthony and Joanne to explain to them that I had something urgent and was going to catch up later in the week. As I drove to my flat, Gianni's car was parked outside. I got out of my car and knocked on his window, he looked up and smiled then he got out and gave me a big hug.

"Mmm, I needed that," I said holding him tighter.

"Are you sure you don't want to cancel? We can go to my parents when Mandy is better," he said.

"No it's okay. Her mom said she would keep me posted. She insisted I come back to you. She sends her congratulations too; she is happy for us," I said cheering up a bit.

We walked into the flat with his arms around me. Once inside, I hurriedly got ready. Gianni asked me to pack an overnight bag as we were staying the night to go to work from there in the morning. We arrived at his parent's just before 9 pm. I was so nervous. I wondered if they would like me and if we would get on. Gianni assured me over and over again not to worry and that they were going to love me; I still couldn't help myself in spite of all his reassurances; I was terrified. I should have had a drink before we left to steady my nerves.

The place was beautiful; it was an elegant house in St. John's wood arranged over three floors. It had spacious entertaining areas, exceptional indoor swimming pool with adjoining leisure area. I guess it was pretty big. They had five bedrooms, three reception rooms, five bathrooms, a garden and patio/terrace.

Wow! I thought Gianni's place was grand but this was superb. After a quick tour of the place, we came back down; his mom and dad were waiting; they were not around when we got to the house. I held Gianni's hand tightly as we walked down the stairs. There was a beautiful red-haired woman in her early forties or so; elegantly dressed in a classy black Michael Kors knee-length dress and a handsome dark hair man, similar age, casually-dressed in blue-and-white-striped Ralph Lauren shirt and Armani black trousers; he looked like Gianni. I turned to Gianni just before we approached them and asked, "I thought you said you are an only child?"

"I am," he replied and looking in the direction of his parents, said, "Mama, Papa..."

His dad, Giovanni, stretched out his arms before he could finish and with a warm smile on their faces, he said, "buongiorno cara come stai?" holding my shoulders and planting a kiss on both of my cheeks. Letting go, he turned to Gianni

"My boy, you did not tell me she was even more beautiful in person."

I started to blush. They looked so young.

"Stop embarrassing the girl, said his mom, Rosa.

"Hello dear," she gave me a hug and a kiss on both cheeks.

"It's so nice to meet you; at last, we have waited a long time for this moment," she said holding my hands. "She is worth the wait, huh?" said Giovanni smiling and nudging his son who nodded in agreement with a look of satisfaction.

"Come on, we will have plenty of time to catch up. I'm sure you are hungry; the food is on the table. I'm afraid we have eaten. We thought you were not coming after what happened to your friend. Is she alright?" asked Rosa concerned.

"She will be," I replied, optimistically as we walked arm in arm toward the dining room where our meal was formally laid out for two with candles and a bouquet of flowers in the center of the table — very romantic, I thought.

Half way through our meal, the 10 o'clock news was on and Gianni was a bit shifty and kept looking over the television across to the lounge where his parents were listening to the news headlines.

"Is everything alright?" I asked turning around to see what he was looking at.

"Mm-hmm" he replied unpersuasively then he called out to his mom "Mama, can you turn the T.V. down, please?"

"I take it you have not told her then?" she questioned.

"Told me what?" I asked curiously.

"It's a surprise," he replied in a modest manner.

After dinner, we joined Giovanni and Rosa in the lounge and we got to know each other a little bit more. Still, I felt that there was something they were hiding from me. By 11:45 pm, I was ready to go to bed as it was going to be my first day back to work and I was especially looking forward to it because I was free to express my feelings and affection towards Gianni publicly. Gianni's parents wanted me to stay for the week so we could get to know one another better and to start planning the wedding preparations. Gianni and I have not set a date yet but I got the feeling he wanted us to wed as soon as possible and so did his parents. They felt we had wasted enough time already.

"Are you sure you have to go tomorrow?" Rosa inquired.

"Yes, I'm afraid so; I kind of left in a hurry to New York," looking over at Gianni shyly holding his hand.

"I had to reschedule all my appointments. I have some unfinished business to tie up not to mention the upcoming office annual ball," I said.

"You work too hard dear, you have to take care of yourself, huh?" She said stroking my facing lovingly like a mother to her child.

There was something so warm and peaceful about her. There was such love in her eyes I felt a connection with her. Instinctively, I knew we would get on and she would be an amazing mother-in-law; all I could do was smile.

"Not like that lazy gold-digger ex-girlfriend of yours, Gina; I don't know why you haven't gotten rid of her, son..." said Giovanni, stopping abruptly as his wife shot him a sharp look and Gianni looking uncomfortable.

Clearing his throat, he clarified, "What I was trying to say is that in the three years you have been with the UK firm, the profits have gone up exceedingly. You pulled in so many top clients in such a short period of time and made positive changes to the firm not to mention making a name for yourself in the public relations world. You are a force to reckon with globally. All the reports we get from all the branches are good."

"You flatter me, Mr. Canuti," I said but before I could continue, he cut in raising his voice slightly in excitement.

"Credit where credit is due!" he said and continued, "We have never in the history of the company had anyone work as hard as you or cared for the firm as much as you have."

"Except for you, of course, when you first started, to prove to your dad that you can stand on your own feet," said Rosa smiling lovingly at her husband.

"Mama, Papa, we have to be heading to bed now; it is late. We will come for dinner after work," said Gianni.

"Is that alright?" Turning to check with me. I nodded in agreement.

As we stood up to go to bed, his mom and dad stood too, "I trust my son has shown you the guest room?" She asked.

Looking puzzled as I wondered what she meant, "My mom is a bit old fashioned," said Gianni smiling.

I made a face and mouthed "oh" biting my lower lip. Rosa hit Gianni playfully with the back of her hand on his arms.

"Don't mind my son," she said to me.

"I believe we all have moral obligations to do the right thing. While I cannot tell you what to do out there...." pointing outside "...but under my roof, however, I cannot allow you to commit fornication because it's against my religious belief but once you are married no problem," she explained.

She gave me a hug and a kiss. I looked at Gianni with my eyes opened wide taking in what she had just said. I kissed the dad then we all said goodnight. Gianni and I left them downstairs and went to bed. It was strange lying in bed on my own with Gianni two doors away from me. I could not sleep as I was missing him terribly. We kept sending each other texts like teenage kids, ultimately his mom and dad went up to bed. We waited for them to fall asleep so we could be together. Gianni attempted to sneak into my room but just as he walked past his parents' bedroom door and was about to enter mine, I heard his mom's voice call out sternly.

"Gianni Spencer Canuti, get back to your room!"

I burst out laughing in my room; she seemed to know her son very well, I thought. For the rest of the night I made fun of Gianni about his middle name, Spencer; texting ourselves until we both fell asleep.

Gianni and I were the first to arrive in the office as always, followed by my wonderful secretary, Annabel. The whole office was buzzing with activities in no time. I noticed that many of them kept looking up at my office once they came in as well as Gianni's which was next to mine. I'm sure if something bad happened in the office, Annabel would call me in New York to tell me. She was the only one who knew where I was, I thought. I buzzed Annabel to bring two coffees for us in Gianni's office followed by her giving us an update for the past two weeks. I got up to go to Gianni's office to find out if he noticed the staring.

When I opened the door, he looked up and smiled, content and happy to see me. I smiled back walking over to his desk.

"Hello Spencer," I said teasing him.

"Come here you," he said grabbing and pulling me to his lap.

We giggled and kissed lovingly at our newly-found freedom and being together publicly. Still sitting on his lap, I asked him if he noticed the workers looking up at our offices. He said that he had not noticed because he had his mind on other things. He ran his left hand to the back of my hair and gave me a seductive kiss.

"Why, Mr. Canuti, you have one track mind," I said blinking innocently.

"Can I help it if I find my fiancée irresistible?" he said with a puppy look eyes.

"According to your mom, we have to refrain from such temptations until after the wedding," I reminded him.

"She said, 'not under her roof'," he replied mischievously.

"You are a bad influence," I said smiling and tugging his chin.

"And you wouldn't want me any other way," he replied.

We both leaned forward to kiss but there was a knock at the door, interrupting.

"Come in," I called out still sitting on Gianni's lap.

It was Annabel with our coffee. She placed them on the table.

"Can I get you anything else?" She asked.

"No, that would be all for now. Thanks," I said.

She stood there with her hands together beaming with happiness. I wondered what was up but I didn't have to wait long.

"Can I just say, I think it's great that you two have finally got together; I mean you make such a wonderful couple," she expressed.

"Also, can I congratulate you.........?"

"Thank you, Annabel! We really appreciate you congratulating us getting together at last I totally agree with you about us make a wonderful couple." Gianni said clearing his throat and cutting her off abruptly. He pushed me off him gently and stood up.

"We have a meeting with one of our clients who insist on seeing both of us urgently; we must leave now. He is expecting us," ushering her out.

"What? Which client and what is it about?" I asked once Annabel left the office perplexed.

"I will fill you in on the way. We must leave now," he said with urgency in his voice. When we both emerged from his office, the workers started clapping for us; unsure what was going on, I looked at Gianni and Annabel for answers. Gianni shrugged his shoulders.

"They are happy for the two of you finally getting together, everyone is," Annabel answered. I was really touched. I looked around at everyone smiling until my eyes caught Gina's hateful stare.

"Not everyone," I acknowledged. Annabel and Gianni followed my gaze and saw her vengeful scowl.

"I wouldn't worry too much about her," Annabel said then she went back to her desk. Some people were coming over to shake Gianni's hand.

"We have to get going," he said ambiguously.

"Yeah sure, let me just grab my things," I insisted walking to my office.

On the corridor was Gianni and Gina's voices, tense and unfriendly; as I approached, I stopped to listen wondering what they were arguing about. Gina had her back to me and Gianni was not aware of my presence.

"She still doesn't know, huh?" she speculated.

"Keep out of this if you know what is good for you," warned Gianni.

"You are not in any position to threaten me, Gianni. If you could have sacked me, you would have done it years ago so if you want me to keep your precious secret, you better be nice to me," she taunted, stroking his face; he quickly pushed her hand away disgusted by her touch.

He grabbed her arm roughly, "Stay away from Sandra or…" he ordered inauspicious manner.

"Or what?" She panted freeing her arm from his grip.

Gianni then spotted me watching. Feeling perturbed, he walked towards me. Gina turned too and frowned at me. She then walked back to her workstation. Gianni took my arms protectively and we left the building without saying a word. When I could no longer stand it, I asked him what was going on.

"Not here, Cara," he said all frazzled.

I didn't say a word because I have never seen him that angry before; not even when we had a fall out. There was a long silence in the car journeying to God knows where. He pulled over all of a sudden, held the steering wheel with both hands and tossed his head back. He took a deep breath then turned to me and took my hand. He could hardly look at my face and his hands were sweaty. He looked so nervous which got me worried.

"You know I love you very much; you are my life," he affirmed.

My face sank and a million images and thoughts flashed before me. Why was he telling me that? What did he do that was so bad to get him worked up like that? What had Gina got over him? Did he cheat on me? Why has he been so edgy for the past couple of days? I knew something was wrong and I wished he could just come out with it.

"Sandra," I heard him call out my name breaking my thoughts.

"Are you listening?" Unable to speak, I just shook my head; then he continued.

"I know you love beautiful clothes and beautiful things as you should. You are a very beautiful woman and being a model, sorry ex-model, you have an eye for fashion and know a designer outfit from a fake one," giving a nervous laugh.

"I love all this about you. It is what makes you, you. Yet I feel like without all the beautiful clothes and things you will still be the same Sandra," looking into my eyes and stroking my hand tenderly.

"What would you say if I told you that the recession hit our firms badly and we lost everything, totally bankrupt, not a penny to my name; everything my family and I own belong to the bank. How would you feel about that? Would you still love me? Would you still want to marry me?" he asked almost pleading with his eyes.

I took my hand back from him and he slouched back to his seat disappointed. I placed my left hand to my chest relieved that it was not any of the stuff I was thinking about. I placed my right hand over my engagement ring stroking it then I took it off and gave it to him. There was a look of fear and utter disappointment in his eyes.

"Keep your ring, I don't want it," he said coldly.

"No, listen please, if we are going to be husband and wife, you need to let me be there for you, for richer or poorer, right?"

I said trying to reassure him.

He sat up straight with a beaming smile. Smiling back sympathetically, I took his hand and placed my engagement ring in his palm.

"You can sell the ring," I explained, "It's worth millions. It can clear some of the family debt, plus I have some savings, too. I can also sell some of my things which should keep the business

146

afloat for a while until we think of some other ways to generate some funds. We may be down but we are not out, if it means starting from scratch, so be it. I can always go back to modelling. Take the ring; it's a start."

"You will do all this for me?" he asked as he was moved to tears.

"All this and more if I could. Gianni, you are my life. I love you more than I have ever loved anyone. You are my first and only true love. We can live in a bus shelter for all I care.... you will still be my Prince Charming and still make me feel like a princess," I declared holding his hands.

He gave me a big hug with a sigh of relief; letting go, he looked into my eyes.

"I have been lying to you," he confessed.

"There is no urgent meeting with a client, is there?" I asked interrupting him.

"No," he replied.

My mobile phone rang; it was Mandy, she wanted to see me urgently in the hospital. Before I could find out if all was well, she put down the phone. Fearing the worse, we drove to the hospital immediately. Upon reaching the hospital, we began to get some stares from people as we walked past. When we entered Mandy's room, her mom and dad were sitting there both staring at Gianni as if he was a movie star or something. Mandy's dad got up and introduced himself to Gianni, "Hello, 'I'm William Martins, Mandy's dad," stretching out his hand for a handshake.

Gianni greeted him. As a consequence, the mom rushed forward and stretched out her hand too. "I'm Penny; Penny

Martins, the mom. I am pleased to meet you, Mr. Canuti, I have heard such wonderful things about you," she smiled stroking her hair almost flirtatiously.

Gianni smiled back taking her hand and kissed it. "Nice to meet you. I too have heard wonderful things about you" he nodded politely.

On the drive back home after leaving Anthony's place, the whole incident in Mandy's room at the hospital played back in my mind.

"Alright.... enough with the pleasantries," Mandy whined, "What's this I hear about you two being engaged? Not only that, I have to hear it from the news report," waving the newspaper at us.

Shocked by what she had just said, I walked over to her and snatched the paper from her to see, forgetting she was still fragile. There was a picture of Gianni and me on the front page. I read the headlines and a bit more but I was unable to believe what I had just read. I flopped down on the chair with my mouth wide opened.

"I can't believe that your Gianni Canuti is 'The Gianni Canuti'. The only son of 'The Canuti Family,' one of the richest Italian mafia families in the world," Mandy blurted out in excitement. "My best friend is engaged to marry him. Wow! How exciting is that!" she added.

I looked up at Gianni who was biting his lower lip and looking at me with concern. I glanced back at the newspaper still in disbelief. I looked at Mandy who was over the moon with the news and stood up slowly, letting the newspaper drop to the ground and walked towards the door dumbstruck by this revelation.

"What, she didn't know?" I heard Mandy asking.

"No," replied Gianni in a somber tone as he followed me out.

Once we were in the car, he started to explain but I told him to just take me home and the rest of the journey was a silent one. When we reached my house, I opened the car to get out. He called my name; I paused but could not look at him. "I love you," he said with insecurity in his voice.

Without responding, I got out and closed the car door not looking back. Once inside my flat, I shut the door behind me and pressed my back against it.

Moments later I took off my shoes and jacket, dropped my handbag on the chair and went straight to pour a stiff drink of cognac for myself. I clenched my teeth and shut my eyes tightly feeling the burning sensation down my throat and chest. Once the burning stopped, I poured another large one, this time, sitting down on the chair and swinging it back and forth. I turned on the T.V flicking through the channels until one station caught my eyes. I turned up the volume — the news was about the engagement of Gianni Canuti, the only grandson of the mafia boss, Luciano Canuti.

I went and poured more drink for myself. I flopped down on my sofa and stared up at the ceiling. My head began to spin; whether it was the drink or information overload, I could not tell. I shut my eyes and wished for the past two days when I had no idea who Gianni was. His mom and dad seemed so nice, how did I miss this? Suddenly, everything began to make sense; each time we went to restaurants or hotels anywhere, they treated him in a most deferential manner. Come to think of it; his mom's name, Rosa, must be the name they had given the hotel, Rosa, in New York where we stayed. That would explain the special treatments we received throughout our stay. I sat up suddenly flabbergasted. Digesting that process of thought, I started to tremble inside.

I gulped not sure how to feel. I got up to get another shot of cognac. As I held the glass, my hand was shaking; images of our last night in New York was plaguing my mind and Gianni shielding me from seeing the news up until then. Why did he lie to me? How could he look me in the eye and lie all these years? Anger started to bubble inside of me. I knocked back my drink, grabbed my handbag, got my shoes on, and stormed out to go and confront him. I struggled to open the door to my car with the key dropping to the ground as my hand was quivering. I supported myself leaning against the car helplessly; I began to cry. Then I felt someone behind me. I turned around quickly almost jumpy. It was Gianni. He picked up my car keys holding it out to me looking remorseful.

"You had no right to keep this from me," I said sobbing, angry and hurt.

"I'm sorry," he apologized moving close to comfort me. I pulled back still angry.

"You lied to me," I said with tears in my eyes.

"I'm really sorry," he repeated repentantly.

Choked up with my tears, I could hardly get the words out "Wh...wh...why?" I croaked.

Before he could answer, I put my hand up to stop him. "You know what? I thought I could do this now but I can't, I can't do this. I need some space; I need to be on my own; I need to think," I said with tears streaming down my cheeks.

I took my car keys from his hand and went back inside not looking back.

Chapter Nine

Facing a Painful Future

By evening, I was feeling a little better after my long cry and a little nap. I made something to eat, had a shower and called Tracey to tell her about Gianni and me being engaged though she might have heard already. When I spoke to her, as always, she understood and saw both sides of the story and advised me to forgive him and not to be too hard on him. I always felt better whenever I talked to Tracey. I really needed to make more time for her though she was pretty preoccupied with her church but she never failed to make time for me. I called Joanne next, but she couldn't pick up. She must have been quite ticked off with me though she was not one to hide her feelings, normally. I knew I had to tell Anthony face to face; I couldn't tell him over the phone and I knew for him to find out in the news like that would be a devastating blow.

I decided to drive to his place and was there before 9 pm. I saw Joanne's car parked next to Anthony's. I thought perhaps she heard the news and had gone to tell him. I pressed the buzzer, no reply. I pressed again and again persistently knowing fully well they were inside. Then I heard Anthony's voice yelling, "Hold your horses, I'm coming." He opened the door half-naked with his hair messed up. He was shocked for seeing me. He stood there and unable to speak.

"Expecting pizza delivery?" I asked sardonically pushing past him.

"I didn't think that was Joanne's style," handing over the bottle of red wine I brought.

"I'll get the glasses, shall I?"

I headed off towards the kitchen. Anthony followed me looking like a child that was caught with his hand in a cookie jar. I took two wine glasses turned to him still holding the wine.

"Well, aren't you going to open it? We have so much to talk about, don't you agree?"

He couldn't look me in the eye. He shuffled off to get the corkscrew to open the wine. I went back to the sitting room then called out to Joanne towards the bedroom.

"It's alright; you can come out now. I know you're in there. We're all friends, after all, right?" I said bitterly feeling the weight of betrayal by the ones I loved the most.

Anthony came out with the wine as Joanne emerged looking pitiful and ashamed unable to look at me. She glanced at Anthony who quickly turned away both feeling highly uncomfortable.

"You needn't have dressed on my behalf," she wrapped her hands around her body wishing she could just disappear.

I turned to Anthony and said calmly, "Be a gentleman and pour me a glass; will you," he hurriedly poured the wine handing it over to me.

"Come on, Anthony; where is yours?" I asked lifting up my glass. "You know I don't like to drink alone with people around."

He filled his own glass reluctantly then I turned to Joanne, "Sorry, Joanne, you have to get your own glass if you want some. If I had known you would be here, I would have brought two bottles."

I drank the whole large glass of wine and with a cynical laughter, l said, "Then again if you knew I was coming, you wouldn't be here. Oops, busted!"

I thrust my empty glass in front of Anthony for a refill. He poured more for me. As I took it, I noticed his glass was still full.

"You are not drinking, Anthony," I said in an indignant tone.

He took a sip of his wine while Joanne said insipidly, "I think I would go now"

"Oh, don't leave on my account," I said acerbically.

"No, err......I think it is best I go," she said timidly.

"You think? You think? Make up your mind girl; it's either you are going or you are staying but then again you could never quite make up your mind, Joanne; could you, huh?" I said, raising my voice and moving towards her.

She looked timorous in her small body frame so I backed away taking a sip of my wine.

"You are never satisfied with what you have. You always want everything I have but as always, you are one step behind. Gianni would never look at you twice; he would see through your foolish games," I said casting a glare over at Anthony disapprovingly.

I went over to Joanne stroking her face with my nail as if slicing it.

"What is it, huh, you want to be me? You wish to be me, right? Well, you can't," I yelled on her face.

"Now sit down. You will go when I say you can go," I said coldly.

She moved swiftly and sat down on the sofa. I turned to Anthony and said, "And you, Mr. Wilson," as I approached him, he looked scared and unsure of what I would do, I don't think I have ever seen him frightened before, "What can I say, only that you are a pathetic, weak man that got caught in the honey trap. She caught you at your weakest moment and you fell into temptation. No doubt; she has been baiting you for a while waiting for the right time to strike." I stroked his cheek lovingly.

"My dear…dear Anthony, I am so sorry it came to this, I never meant to hurt you. I can only but imagine how you must be feeling right now," I said tormenting him a little and walking around him.

"Didn't your Bible warn you to flee from immoral women, mmm…let me see," I placed my index finger upon my lips thinking.

"Oh yes! In Proverbs somewhere it says, 'Love wisdom like a sister; make insight a beloved member of your family. Let them protect you from an affair with an immoral woman, from listening to the flattery of a promiscuous woman.' I guess you don't love wisdom enough, huh? What else does it say? 'Seductively dressed and sly of heart. She was the brash, rebellious type, never content to stay at home. So she seduced him with her pretty speech and enticed him with her flattery. He

156

followed her at once like an ox going to the slaughter. He was like a stag caught in a trap, awaiting the arrow that would pierce its heart. He was like a bird flying into a snare, little knowing it would cost him his life.'"

I looked over at Joanne who sat there hugging her knees terrified of what I might do. I turned my attention back to Anthony who was also fretful.

"Don't worry. I'm not going to kill you" I said pacing up and down.

"Go and get some clothes on," I commanded Anthony. At first, he was reluctant to leave but seeing my countenance, he left. I walked over to Joanne who kept looking nervously over the direction that Anthony went.

"If I wanted to hurt you, he won't be able to do anything about it. You can relax." I sat down next to her; exhausted by all the things that had happened in a space of two days. I rubbed my temple then turned to her and said, "We are supposed to be friends. You've gone too far this time; you have crossed the line." She lowered her head remorsefully.

"You realize he couldn't care less about you, don't you? He's just using you to get back at me. I know you really like him. I saw the way you were looking at him in the hospital yesterday though you tried to hide it." She started to cry.

"Your tears will not save you this time. I don't think we can come back from this; you must really hate me," I said feeling sad because I valued our friendship.

"No, I don't hate you Sandra, I hate myself; I hate me, me!" She said crying uncontrollably.

Unmoved by her tears I got up and poured myself another glass of wine and drank. Anthony came back wearing dark blue jeans and a white t-shirt. He looked over at Joanne who was still crying with her head bowed down in shame. I handed Anthony his drink which he gladly took and drank. He stood there awkwardly, unsure what to say or do so I said to Joanne callously, "Leave us and get out! I will deal with you later."

She jumped up so fast and couldn't wait to leave. She grabbed her things and left without saying a word. Anthony stood there looking so nervous. I felt sorry for him so I walked over and gave him a lingering kiss on the lips. I could feel him relaxing a bit so I stopped and pulled away gently.

"I am sorry," I said to him apologetically.

"No, I am sorry. I didn't know what I was thinking; I don't even like Joanne, and she is a rich spoilt brat who wouldn't leave me alone. She kept calling and always hanging around. Can you believe she even came to church with me one morning? She is a woman who does not take no for an answer. I know that is no excuse and I take full responsibility for being weak. Hand on heart, this is the first time it's ever happened. She came over with the newspaper rubbing it in about your engagement to golden boy," he said; referring to Gianni as he babbled on like he did when he was nervous.

I rolled my eyes showing my displeasure because he knew I didn't like it when he called Gianni golden boy as an insult. When he noticed things were getting serious with Gianni and me, our relationship started to deteriorate though it was platonic. We did not see or call each other as often as we used to; that's mainly my fault because he had always been there for me. I guess deep down he felt he and I would be the ones to get married someday.

"I didn't mean for you to find out like that," I said; rubbing his arm tenderly.

I went to the mini bar and took out a bottle of Pinot Grigio rose and started to open it. He took it from me, opened and poured it for both of us. We sat down on the black leather sofa — a lot more relaxed. I looked at him and let out a deep sigh wondering why this wonderful, kind, loving and patient man that I had put through so much over the years kept coming back for more hurt.

"Why won't you let me go?" I asked caressing his face.

"Simple; I love you and I don't know how to stop," he said gazing into my eyes.

I lowered my head feeling pain and sadness for him because he deserved someone who could love him back the way he loved me; he was a good-looking and loving man but I didn't feel the same way about him. Yes, I loved him but not the same way that I loved Gianni. With Gianni, it is fireworks and sparks but with Anthony, it's cocoa and pyjamas though it wasn't always that way. I leaned my head on his shoulders and he held me tight. We sat there in silence for a while as if we knew this was goodbye.

"I've lost you for good this time, haven't I?" he asked.

I could not answer in fear that if I opened my mouth, I would start crying but I did not need to answer because he already knew. He tightened his grip slightly placing his face on my head.

My mobile phone started ringing bringing me back to the present. I looked at it, Gianni's name and the photo were

159

flashing. I turned it off and leaned back on Anthony's shoulder. He knew it was Gianni then he shifted on his seat facing me.

"I've got to ask; did you ever love me? I mean I know you did, I felt you did even though in all the years we were together you never told me that you loved me. I know with your upbringing it was hard for you to say it then but now I really need to know," he asked holding his breath.

"Yes I did, I still do in a way but different," I replied earnestly.

"Not like golden boy; sorry, Gianni," he said.

"You were my first love, my knight in shining armor. You were always there for me picking up the pieces and bandaging my wounds. I didn't even stop to think of your broken heart. I have been so selfish over the years; I am so sorry," I said regretfully.

"No, you were young. I knew you needed to have your freedom to experience life. If I had tried to hold you tight, I would have lost you for good," he said; his eyes still filled with love and compassion.

"You will never lose me," I said snuggling up closer to him. We sat there in silence until I fell asleep in his arms there on the sofa.

The next day, I woke up on the sofa covered with a blanket. I smiled thinking of how thoughtful and loving Anthony was and hoped that one day God would bless him with a good wife who was going to love and take care of him the way he deserved to be treated. I saw a note on the table saying, "Sorry, had to go to work,. Will call you later. Love, Anthony." I had a shower then made breakfast for myself. I cleaned up and then left. I drove around for a while unsure what to do with myself. I called Tracey and asked her to meet me at the hospital in Mandy's room. I asked her to call Joanne so both of them would come but she was not to let her know I was going be there. I gave them a time to arrive in the hospital.

When I opened the door and went in, I stared directly at Joanne who jumped immediately on seeing me. I walked closer and kissed Tracey and Mandy. Greeting them, I sat down opposite Joanne who refused to make eye contact with me. Tracey and Mandy sensed the tension between us since neither of us was saying anything. Mandy, unable to wait any longer, burst out asking what the problem was.

"Ask Joanne," I told her knowing Joanne would be too ashamed to talk.

I ended up telling them everything; unable to believe what they had just heard, Mandy asked me to repeat what I had just said.

"You heard me," I said folding my arms.

Tracey walked over to Joanne with a look of unbelief, "Please tell me this is not true, and it is a joke, right?" She asked hoping that Joanne would deny it.

Joanne kept her head down and did not answer. Tracey came to me and asked if what I saw was real.

"Not only did I catch them red-handed, they both confirmed it. She thinks she is in love with Anthony and wants to step in my shoes," I said sarcastically expressing disapproval.

"Just the thought of it is giving me a headache; ouch, ouch!" said Mandy adjusting herself on the bed and all of us jumped simultaneously to her aid fussing over her.

For a moment, we forget about our fall out but as soon as we were sure Mandy was fine, our faces changed, especially Mandy's, who told Joanne to get off her.

"I don't need your help if you can do this to your best friend. I hate to see what you would do to your enemies. How could you stoop so low? You can have any man you want; I don't get you. I have watched you compete stupidly with Sandra over the years and it seems to get worse and worse. Now see where it has landed you. You claim not to have any real friends. If this is how you treat them, are you surprised? I can't believe you have done this. Jo, I just can't believe it," she said disappointedly.

Tracey sat at the edge of the bed letting out a sigh. She turned to Joanne.

"You have crossed the line this time, Joanne. You have really crossed the line. Anthony must really hate himself right now. It's hard enough for him dealing with losing Sandra to Gianni. You go over there like Jezebel and cause the man to sin; that is heartless," said Tracey sorrowfully.

Tracey got up from the bed angrily rubbing her hands together in agitation, "I am truly sorry but I can't be in the same room with you right now, I have to go. I will come and see you, Mandy, before visiting hours is over later. Sandra, I will give you a ring to make sure you're okay," she just looked over at Joanne briefly who was crying, then left.

"I don't think I have ever seen Tracey this upset before," said Mandy looking at the door.

"She and Anthony are good friends and they are both committed Christians; what Joanne did in her eyes is very evil.

162

If you remember years back, Anthony stopped sleeping with me because he became born-again. Unless you are married, it is called fornication; which is a sin," I said explaining to Mandy who knew from those times when I got frustrated of his rejection whenever I made sexual advances at him. I ended up having one night stands with men to satisfy my sexual urges. Joanne knew this as well and continued to push him until she wore him down.

My phone rang; I went to answer it. It was Anthony; he wanted to know if I could meet him for lunch so I agreed to meet him at his place of work. I left Mandy and Joanne after kissing Mandy. I was glad that Mandy was feeling better. We had not sat down to catch up properly. I still didn't know exactly what happened between her and Aden. I wanted her to recover fully and come out of the hospital before I brought it up.

I arrived at Anthony's workplace and as I was walking past the nurse's station, the black girl I saw him kiss years ago came over and congratulated me on my engagement to Gianni. She was overly friendly towards me. I gave her an unfriendly smile and walked past her. I could hear her giggling behind me. I went to Anthony's office and we embraced and kissed. He told me that he was still ashamed of what he and Joanne did but he asked God to forgive him and help him move on. Then he told me that Tracey called and they prayed together. He said that his parents were very disappointed about my engagement to Gianni as they already took me as their daughter-in-law. I felt so bad. We sat in the office awkwardly for a while then we went for lunch.

During lunch, we had a heart-to-heart conversation and resolved to remain good friends and concluded that we met too early and that if we were meeting now as adults, things could have turned out differently. I wished him well and asked him to move on with his life but if he ever needed me for anything, I would always be there for him. He watched me drive off, waving. I felt pain in my heart; tears ran down my face. I felt like I had lost part of me but I knew that we had to part forever and get on with our lives.

'How sure am I this time; now that matters are on the rocks with Gianni?' I questioned myself, knowing full well that it is not the first time Anthony and I had gone our separate ways to come back together in the end. 'Come to think of it, will I have to let Gianni go too?'

The Sequel

MY LOVE, MY HEART

Euphemia Chukwu